The Molotov Cocktail

Prize Winners Anthology

Vol. 2

Edited by Josh Goller

The Molotov Cocktail

Copyright © 2016 Accelerant Publishing
Portland, Oregon

www.themolotovcocktail.com

Rights to individual pieces belong to their respective authors.

Editor: Josh Goller
Associate Editor: Mary Lenoir Bond
ISBN: 1540713245
ISBN-13: 978-1540713247

Contents

	Acknowledgments	i
1	Monsters	2
2	Phenomena	38
3	Felons	74
4	Shadows	108
5	Icons	130

Acknowledgments

The Molotov Cocktail is a projectile for explosive flash fiction (and occasionally a little poetry), the kind of writing that's cooked up in a bathtub and handled with rubber gloves. Published roughly twice monthly since 2010, we crave dark and offbeat flash fiction, full of rotten characters, strange and surreal occurrences, and a spot or two of blood.

You now hold in your hands our second annual Prize Winners Anthology print issue. This is the culmination of a year's worth of contests, which were filled with Monsters, Phenomena, Felons, Shadows, and Icons. The past year saw us establish our first-ever poetry contest and mega-issue, which we plan to make an annual event. Once again we were bowled over by the quality of writing we received not only for our contests, but for our regular issues as well.

We want to thank each writer who has ever submitted to our journal. Without you, we literally couldn't do this. We also want to thank you, dear reader, for choosing the kind of path that not only led you to this book but also for developing an appreciation for the gloriously weird that allows the gonzo imagery contained herein to find a cozy home nestled in your grey matter.

Monsters

The Testimony of the Accused

By Colin Rowe

Nestled among the autumn wheat, I saw a milk snake eating a black toad. Only the toad's head was sticking out, but his black eyes searched and blinked. I was hunched over, sickle in hand, cutting the crop one handful at a time in mindless repetition, and I might have sliced them both if the toad had not made himself known.

"Kill your family," said the toad.

"What?"

"Kill your parents and your little brother and kill the dog too."

"Why the dog?"

"Because I asked you to."

"Do you want some help? I could kill this snake."

"Kill your family," said the toad.

Awake all night, I rubbed my blistered hands together under the blankets and tried to stop their shaking. There were as many grasshoppers in the bush outside my window as there were stars in the calm, cloudless sky. How could anyone sleep with that noise? I looked at my brother in the bed across the room, dreaming, worryless, drooling on his arm. I rose from the bed and put on my shoes.

The sickle was where I left it, hung in the barn with the others like artwork in a private gallery. When I took it from its hook, my hands stopped shaking.

The bush was the problem. The bush was full of grasshoppers. Noisy, stupid grasshoppers. They congregated there to chirp and screech and didn't care who they kept awake. The dry branches of the bush were nearly leafless, but looked full from a distance. They were populated with a hundred thousand angular, pointy insects, their carapaces shiny in the blue moonlight. I shouldered the branches away to expose the main stem, and the grasshoppers panicked at my touch, hopped away, high and low, landed on my back, skittered up my arms, became tangled in my hair.

I gripped the stem and chopped it, pulled upward and felt the plant give way just a little with each fresh cut. Greenwood juice spilt from the wound until there was a great crack and splinter. I stood and hoisted the upturned bush by its stem. The roots left in the ground wriggled and screamed as they vanished into the dirt.

The last leaves fell off the bush, then the branches, and then it was a snake. The stem was a milk snake that I grasped in my hand. It coiled about my wrist like a friend, and my brother said, "What are you doing?"

His head was poking out the window and my sickle was through his throat before I looked. His body slumped over the sill. Dark blood poured from his throat, washed down the side of the house, and filled the place where the bush had been with a shimmering black pool.

"Now your parents," said the snake. I loosed my grip on the reptile and it wound itself up my arm and around my neck where it stayed, cold and dry, whispering into my ear with its probing tongue.

I opened their throats as they slept, as easily as unlacing a boot. Father coughed and sputtered, spraying red spittle into my unblinking face. The noise woke mother. She shouted something before I killed her, but I can't remember what.

The dog didn't bleed. He was tied up outside, barking a terrible racket and when I cut his throat the voice escaped. The howling, barking, whimpering voice of confusion and dread spilled out like the blood that should have. It covered my hands in warm, wet void.

Hours passed in the world and a lifetime passed in my soul. The sun was rising pink and red through the treetops and the horizon was an elsewhere world; a place of peace and mysteries and power. The silhouettes of the branches on the sunrise were the black stripes on the milk snake. Black, red, black, yellow, black, red, black, yellow.

"What do I do now?" I asked the snake.

"Die," it said. A brown hawk snatched the milk snake in its yellow talons and flew away from me. The snake hung limp in the air and was carried off, far away, into the world beyond the sky.

Hang me, if you must.

#

Colin Rowe has been published in dozens of magazines and co-hosts Short Short Stories, a live reading event in Santa Fe, NM. He tweets under the handle @lowericon and the first chapter of his upcoming novel, *The Red Bear*, can be found in *Aurora Wolf* magazine.

Come Home, Sweetheart

by Cassandra A. Clarke

I was never one for going to mass on Sunday, though I tried to be. My parents were that kind of people. It never stuck with me. I always stared at the stained glass too long, rearranging the shapes and shards of red to resemble another picture. Once, I swear, the glass looked like the taut legs of can-can dancers underneath silken skirts. They were laughing; their mouths hidden by the arc of window.

There was never anything inside a church for someone like me, an architect by trade, a grown woman who likes to break things down and rebuild them to maximize space, talk, and movement. Churches aren't those kind of things. But still, I am running towards my childhood church. I don't know what I expect to find there, beneath the multi-colored glass, those kicking legs, those lines of pews arranged to make me feel how inaccessible God was from my seat.

I was visiting my parents. Or, really, my father.

My dad had gotten old. Old enough that he often forgot where he was and who he was. Mom decided that she needed a trip. Didn't say where she was going or when she'd be back.

Just smiled at me, and squeezed me so tight that her Chanel perfume made me sneeze on her shoulder.

Dad was on our lawn. He was mowing it. He stopped. He looked at the sky, as if he heard something I couldn't. I saw him from the window. His head cranked back like a duckling. I went out to see if he was okay, or if he needed a glass of water. I was new to this, caretaking. I didn't know what to ask.

I touched his shoulder. When I did, he spun around. I leapt back in shock, and felt ashamed.

His eyes, which typically had a sheen of white covering his irises like a veil, looked even whiter than I remembered. His head shook side to side. His teeth, those gloriously crooked teeth, sugar-stained from sneaking chocolate syrup into his cereal each morning, snarled at me.

"It's ok," I said to him, although I knew I was really saying it for myself.

His teeth gnashed at me like I wish a piece of chum in the ocean and he was the shark that had always been watching me underneath the waves. I wondered if this was what age was like. If it waited for us all like this, until we were too weak to push it away.

He approached me, reaching his hands out for my throat. It couldn't really be him, I thought. He's having a spell, I guessed.

Spell or him or old age or wonder did me no good. He still reached out to grab me by my collar. His yellowed nails scratched the spot above my collarbone. I could feel the wet trickle of blood. He opened his mouth and on his tongue I saw three bottle-caps from soda. He wasn't allowed to drink Coke because it made him cranky. There was the Coke insignia, laced in blood, as if he chewed the bottle whole.

I wish I could have been the person to wrap my arms around him and wait until the thing that was inside him lulled. I wish I kissed his forehead. Instead, I ran to the church.

Inside, the church was empty. Lanterns were lit near the pulpit. Flowers were standing by the door in attention. Lilies. I stopped to touch one. Mom always said if you touched one, it would bruise. I touched one, but these didn't. I ripped the petals from the stalk, and stamped onto them.

Outside, I could see him approaching. Our church was only a block away from our house. He would find me. He would shake me until I threw up onto the tile floor.

I looked to the rows of pews, each one so bare and open, and I envied them for their inability to want shelter. I walked to the nearest one and sat down. I could hear the doors rattle open, and could hear the sound of the thing that was and wasn't my father approach. He was mine now to watch. I looked to the stained glass windows and this time found one painted in differing hues of blue. The window looked to be a sky cracking in half, cracking right where the dove met the horizon, as if begging to be broken.

#

Cassandra A. Clarke's work has been previously published (or upcoming) at: *Electric Literature*, *Word Riot*, *Cartridge Lit* and other speculative places. She's the Chief Editor of the new-weird literary magazine, *Spectator & Spooks* and a proud member of the Pug Squad writing collective. When not writing, Cassandra can be found training at her dojang, Jae H. Kim Taekwondo, in Cambridge, MA.

Brother Stone

By Manuel Royal

Saturdays I visit Louisa's grave with a three-pound hammer and flowers. Hibiscus, her favorite.

Disappointment has a smell. It's soaked into my pores, like the smell of eight hundred thousand Luckies in Louisa's leathery skin. She had a deep regret for giving birth to me. When I was little she squinted down at me through blue smoke, shook her head slow, that candy-red mouth grimacing around a lipsticked, unfiltered smoke.

I guess she would've aimed that load of disappointment at my father if he'd been around. I took it in the face, standing in for him.

Nathaniel's father was the only good man, that's what she said. I think he was one of the men who came to the house when I was seven, but I was trying first grade again so I was busy and anyway it hurts my head to remember way back.

My brother Nathaniel, the golden child. She knitted lambswool boots for him, a hundred pairs over the years. Sometimes we hadn't any food, but vodka and Luckies and lambswool we had, soft as a moonlit cloud, nothing too good for the golden child.

Stone, not gold, Nathaniel was, for real. A stone. Sometimes a baby grows in the wrong place in a woman. It stops moving and speck by speck it calcifies, turns to a stone inside her.

Stone baby. There's a Greek word, but it just means stone baby. That was Nathaniel. Brother Stone. Not moving; hiding inside her. Not-normal.

Monster.

Louisa crazied up a different Nathaniel in her mind, the picture of health and joy. She wrote up his report cards, all A's. Mother's Day cards from Nathaniel came two hundred days a year. She wrote them, dropped them in the mailbox in front of the smokes shop.

Golden Nathaniel won trophies, being naturally a decathlete with perfect form. I heard all about it every night when I brought her dinner.

Stone Nathaniel stayed in her gut like a statue she swallowed. Sleeping maybe, building up a hideous strength year by year, nine months over and over. Stone-still like a leopard in a tree. Waiting to do bad.

Monster.

I got no trophies. Brought home C's. Look at a graph of schoolwide student performance. See the point marked "Average" — that's me there. That little dot.

I was always where I was supposed to be, doing the expected. Average is normal, that's me. Not Louisa, not Brother Stone.

I graduated and worked every day. Louisa caught me looking at apartment ads and pressed the end of her cigarette into the back of her hand until I promised to never move out.

That left a scar, and, funny story, the day I turned 25 I came home (and made her steak because it was Wednesday) and Louisa came out in her maternity dress and looked up and said, "You've got his face" and she grabbed my head and kissed me, only time ever I think. It tasted like cigarettes and then she gave me the back of her hand, she had to reach way up, she said, "No good!" and swung hard. That rough round scar split my lip.

I never got mad, never. She was not-normal, imaginary golden Nathaniel was inhumanly perfect, gut-stone Nathaniel was a monster waiting to do bad, so I had to be extra-normal all the time to pull the household average closer to that dot, that safe place. So never, I never got angry.

Except one time. I think last year, just once. I'll check the year on the stone Saturday, also I'll bring a new copy of *People* to help remember what this year is (she still gets magazines in the mail, they don't care she's dead).

Right, so one time I got angry and I was bad. I remember it all dark, like dark night inside the house, and nothing but Louisa's white thin face, blue smoke puffing from her red mouth. She said Nathaniel's father Nathan was coming to stay and they'd be together, she and the only good man Nathan and golden Nathaniel, and she expected me to be gone, didn't fit, not good enough.

So that was the one time, and it only lasted ten seconds. But I was pretty mad, and it was Wednesday again so I was pounding the steak thin like Louisa liked and the tenderizer sank into her soft head.

Ten seconds of being bad felt better than a lifetime of being not good enough.

Then my brother spoke to me. Finally. Right from inside of her, after all those silent waiting years. Brother Stone told me what to do.

I went out, locked up and broke into my own house, then broke into six other houses around town and used the same tenderizer on six people. Sorry, seven people, that one guy had a live-in nurse.

Brother Stone's plan. He liked doing bad. Monster. But he was smart and it worked. Case is still unsolved.

I did everything he said except I didn't cut him out of her. I thought Louisa just crazied up Nathaniel's father Nathan, but he showed up for real when they were putting Louisa's box in the ground. Brother Stone kept shouting at me from in the box, said to put Nathan in the hole with him, but I didn't have the tenderizer anymore and anyway they put in the dirt and I couldn't hardly hear Brother Stone anymore.

Nathan went away after that, back to Ohio, but just to be sure I got a three-pound hammer and followed and put him in a quarry. Good enough. Every time I swing a blunt instrument I don't miss. Good enough feels pretty good.

Every Saturday visit I look real close at the dirt because someday Brother Stone will climb up through the dirt. His little stone head will pop out and I'll swing my hammer and do one good thing for the world.

#

Manuel Royal, like Tristram Shandy, was born with a broken nose. He will die. In between, he lives and writes in Atlanta, Georgia.

Beyond the Block

By Aeryn Rudel

The block gleams with congealed blood as I kneel before it. The headsman has been busy today—I'm the last of twenty. He towers over me, and his eyes, a surprising bright blue, gleam from the depths of his black hood. They are twin glaciers where it seems warmth or mercy can find no purchase. He takes one hand from the haft of his axe, places a meaty palm between my shoulder blades, and pushes me over, forcing my neck into the notch. The block is cold on my skin, and it smells of the butcher's stall, coppery and rank.

"Don't squirm," the headsman says, leaning down to whisper into my ear. His breath smells of onions and pipe weed. "Stay still, and the axe will bite clean." It is a kindness, this warning. Today I saw the axe crack the spine of a man who jerked forward to avoid the headsman's stroke. His pained screams still ring in my ears. I will be still.

I stare at the small crowd gathered before the gibbet. It has dwindled now; most have had their fill of death. Lord Magister Vyard is still there, of course, a gaunt scarecrow in black, the three-pronged sigil of his office glaring from his breast, blood red in the fading afternoon sun. Lucinda stands next to him, trying to look away. Vyard's thin fingers are locked around the back of her neck like talons, keeping her facing forward. He wants her to see this. Vyard's lips are moving. I cannot hear what he says, but his mouth twists and draws violently as he utters some silent, hateful curse.

The headsman draws in a deep breath above me, and I hear the honed steel of the axe-head scrape away from the gibbet. The axe whistles down, and there is sudden, terrible pressure on my neck, just below the base of my skull. There is no pain as my head comes cleanly away from my body, just the dizzying terror of the world turning end over end.

My head rolls a few feet and stops, then I hear the heavy tread of the headsman moving in my direction. I open my mouth to speak but can make no sound. The throat and lungs that empowered speech are part of the body sprawled lifeless behind the block.

The headsman's thick fingers twine through my hair, and he hoists me up for the crowd's appreciation. I have a clear view of the executioner's square. I see the crowd, I see Lucinda on her knees before a puddle of vomit, and I see Vyard striding forward. He holds open a black silk bag, and when he reaches the scaffold, the headsman drops me into it.

I plunge into darkness, and here I wait for death. I wait for sight and hearing to fade. I wait to behold the gates of heaven or writhe in the fires of damnation. I experience neither. I come to the strange and awful realization that my head lives apart from my body. This realization is quickly followed by another. Vyard is the Lord Magister, the king's most powerful sorcerer, a man to whom death is a paltry obstacle. For loving Lucinda, Vyard's young wife, he had me executed and now something much worse. The man's rages are feared throughout the kingdom, and his curses are more than angry words.

Light returns as I am pulled from the silk bag. The light is from a torch carried in the left hand of man who is not Vyard. He holds my head in his right. I see a bare stone wall before me, and upon it a row of tall iron spikes. The man lifts me above the wall, and I see the executioner's square below and the city sprawling beyond. The height of my vantage point and the view tells me where I am—the Lord Magister's tower.

There is sudden sharp pressure—again, no pain—as the stump of my neck is forced down onto a spike. The man, a guard perhaps, grunts with the effort of forcing the iron barb through the meat and gristle. His task complete, he leaves me, taking the light of his torch with him.

This is to be my fate, to spend years uncounted as a ghoulish ornament upon my killer's wall. Vyard has condemned me to a hell of slow and certain madness, another victim of the Lord Magister's cruelty.

Before I can slip further into despair, I am aware of a strange sensation. A feeling outside the prison of my skull, like an old memory I can't completely recall. Then it crystalizes, and joy surges through me—I can feel my hands, my legs, my body! At first it is little more than a ghostly tingling, like an itch I can't quite scratch. Then the sensation intensifies, and I feel my fingers moving against soft and yielding resistance. I can see the empty square below and the pile of corpses near the gibbet. I focus on my body, forcing my legs to move, my arms to push. The pile of headless corpses in the square below topples over, and among them is my own.

I tell my body to stand. It obeys my phantom urging, and I can feel solid ground beneath its feet. I carefully pilot my orphaned flesh to the gibbet, mount the stairs, and move to the block where my mortal life ended. I tell my hands to pick it up the headsman's axe, and its dead weight feels like something I have long been without. It feels like power, and it feels like vengeance.

I turn my body toward the Magister's tower. Vyard will come to gloat soon, and when he does, all of me will be waiting for him.

#

Aeryn Rudel is a freelance writer from Seattle, Washington. He is a notorious dinosaur nerd, a rare polearms expert, a baseball connoisseur, and he has mastered the art of fighting with sword-shaped objects (but not actual swords). Aeryn's first novel, *Flashpoint*, was recently published by Privateer Press, and he occasionally offers dubious advice on the subjects of writing and rejection (mostly rejection) on his blog at www.rejectomancy.com.

Decent People

By Shawn Campbell

It was a lonely stretch of the Yellowhead Highway, fifty kilometers either way to any kind of civilization. The sun sat fat on the western horizon, mostly obscured by evergreen sentinels. The walls of the river canyon fell to the north side of the highway, blanketed by pines and firs broken by the occasional face of jagged rock. The black mass of the Skeena River slid past the south side of the highway. A moving barrier dividing it from the rise of the canyon on the opposite bank.

The car sat facing west. Its hood up and its blinkers on. The man leaned against the side of the car, one hand holding a cigarette and the other keeping to the pocket of his faded coat. The man reclined, smoked, and waited, listening to the sounds of the wind through the trees and the constant gurgle of the river, watching the lengthening stretch of his shadow. He shivered with every burst of wind. It was getting cold. A pile of cigarette butts lay scattered about his feet. The paint of the car was faded and the edges of the fenders were flecked with rust. It was an old car. The man would probably not be having his trouble if it had been a new car, but it was the car he had. No point musing about how things could be different.

A set of headlights crested the hill to the east. A new model pickup truck. Blue. Diesel engine. The gentle roar moved closer, slicing through the twilight air. The man watched the pickup approach. The hand in his pocket tightened. The hand with the cigarette rose into the air. Stop. C'mon stop you mother fucker. The pickup seemed to slow. There you go. Help a poor bastard out.

The pickup didn't stop. It moved halfway across the yellow line and swept past. The man turned his head and covered his eyes to protect them from the buffeting wall of wind. He shivered. The red taillights moved on down the highway. Brake. Hit the brakes, you asshole. Come back. The brake lights stayed dark. The man didn't think they would. The hand in his pocket loosened. He spit on the ground and muttered a few choice curses under his breath. Eight cars in five hours. Not one had stopped. There just weren't any decent people anymore.

Down the highway a deer poked her head out of the undergrowth. An old, dry doe. She took a couple of steps to the edge of the pavement, looked both ways, took another few steps, looked again, and then walked to the other side. The man watched her as she moved. The deer looked rough. Her coat was ragged. Too many ticks and fleas. Her ribs poked through. Poor old bitch. Probably missing half her teeth. Lose those and she was good as dead. Animals don't die from old age. They starve, get eaten, or shit themselves to death. Hell of a way to go. The deer moved out of sight down towards the river. If she was lucky a truck would hit her on the way back.

The man took the last hit from his cigarette and tossed it to the gravel at his feet. He crushed the ember with his worn out shoe. His finger probed at a hole in his jeans and then moved up. His hand rubbed his jaw, rough with stubble. He needed a shave, and his moustache needed a trim. Not important now. No reason to give much thought to problems you can't solve. The wind picked up a bit. Wisps of hair broke loose from their fellows and floated on the breeze.

Twenty years ago there had still been plenty of decent people around. If you saw a broken-down car on the side of the road you stopped and offered to help. You're lucky I came along, not much traffic on this highway. Let me look at that engine for you. Any idea what it is? Do you need a lift into town? Hop on in. No problem at all. Hope somebody would do the same for me. It wasn't that way anymore. Nowadays decent people were far and few between. Maybe he'd head south. He had heard there were still decent people down south. People who didn't judge you by the way you looked or the car you drove.

The man spit again. It was getting late. The sun was below the horizon. The stars were starting to twinkle. It was going to be a beautiful night. Clear as hell out in the middle of nowhere. Probably be able to see the Milky Way. Damn cold though. Too damn cold to be sitting out hoping to get lucky.

The man lifted himself from the car and walked around to the back. He pulled keys out of his pants pocket and opened the trunk. Jug of water, pile of rags, jumper cables, jack, length of rope, duffel bag full of clothes, shovel. He took the short piece of heavy pipe from his coat pocket, placed it on the rags, and shut the trunk. The man walked to the front of the car and closed the hood. He opened the car door and climbed into the driver's seat. He reached behind him and pulled a pistol from the waistband of his pants, nestled against his back. The pistol went into the jockey box.

The man fumbled with his keys and started the car. It coughed and roared to life. The belts squealed. They'd need to be changed soon. The blinkers went off. The headlights went on. The car turned and headed east down the highway. Fifty kilometers to Terrace. He could stay at the Rainbow Inn there. It was cheap. Not nice, but cheap. Tomorrow was another day. The man took a pack of cigarettes off the dash and lit another smoke. It was just so hard to find decent people anymore.

#

Shawn Campbell lives in Oregon with a very nice houseplant named Morton. He currently has a novel called *The Uncanny Valley* available on Amazon.

The Garbage Men

By M.B. Vigil

Silver Street was always one of the cleanest and most peaceful in Sunset Days Retirement Village on Florida's Gulf Coast. We all kept our lawns tidy, our fences mended, and our blinds half shut. In fact, everyone there seemed painfully private. For a same-sex couple, it was ideal. Like most of our neighbors, my partner and I typically retired by ten-thirty and rose shortly after dawn. The only noises after midnight were the odd duck meeting its end in the gator-filled canal and the trash collector/street sweeper team that visited Monday and Thursday mornings between four and five. And the time Geraldine Rosenblum's security alarm malfunctioned at two a.m.

I'd often wake up when the sanitation vehicles rumbled by our house. It was a soothing sound, meditative. Once, I told Patrick it reminded me of the train that rattled the walls of my childhood home at night. Purring by in the wee hours, it would assure me that I was safe in my bed, that my big brother was in the bunk overhead, and that our overprotective grandparents were asleep in the next room. I'd roll over, grab my pillow, and drift back into dreamland.

Oddly, no one in Sunset Days could remember ever paying for trash collection service. Perhaps it was included in the city's water and sewer bill, or else in our property taxes.

When the Edelsteins' granddaughter disappeared one night, nobody was particularly surprised. They found her bedroom window ajar and assumed that she'd run off with her boyfriend again or hitchhiked up the coast, again. She had the reputation of a wild child—tattoos, nose piercing, dark clothing. We all knew she was trouble and decided that Frank and Edna were lucky to be rid of her for the rest of the summer. After the police had concluded their investigation, we all whispered about it within the privacy of our separate abodes.

Unbeknownst to me, Patrick had agreed to take his sister's Chihuahua while she was in Madrid with her fiancée. This would be her third husband, the one who, according to Jackie Onassis, you married for companionship (the first two were for love and money, respectively). I'd married Patrick for love and companionship. We both had had prosperous careers.

Colleen dropped the dog off on a Friday evening. Taquita was an angel throughout the weekend, but she started to become distressed Sunday before bed. At four in the morning, we awoke to the dog barking and scratching at the door. When I stepped outside, she darted between my legs and ran straight for the street, where the garbage truck had just turned onto our block. A golf-cart-sized street sweeper followed closely behind.

Yipping and growling, Taquita chased after the goliath and its sidekick. Today, I'm not sure I didn't imagine it, but at that time I would've sworn that no one sat in the driver's seat of either vehicle. They seemed to move of their own accord, engines growling like ravenous hellhounds, headlights trolling from side to side like giant reptilian eyes. A team of five or six little people in black coveralls (not one of them stood more than four feet tall) hopped off the cart and bustled about with push brooms that seemed too long for their little arms. In spite of the apparent challenge, they swept up behind the procession.

One of the little people signaled with a quiet whistle and pointed at Taquita. In response, a long insect-like arm reached from the side of the garbage truck and snatched her up as I stood dumfounded on the curb. With one crunch, the dog was silenced. Its insides spilled out onto the street, and the arm craned up and held the remains over the back of the truck. With a whoosh, the empty carcass was sucked down into some gaping mechanical maw. The truck emitted a vulgar belch from its exhaust stack while the gaggle of little people hobbled over, set their brooms aside, and dropped to their knees before the splattered offal. Making the most disgusting sounds, they lapped at the ground with their tongues until all signs of Taquita had been, well, cleaned up.

I didn't realize I'd been screaming until the little monsters looked up at me and then around at the neighbors, who stood aghast under the glow of the street lamps. The jig was up. In a unified front, the private, isolated residents of Sunset Days Retirement Village closed in around the night creatures. Frank Edelstein was armed with a shotgun, while his wife screamed obscene accusations at the little people. We were too many for them to fend off. Still, they lashed out defensively with their broomsticks as they jumped back onto their cart. The cart, in turn, rolled up onto a ramp and into the back of the garbage truck. The whole monstrosity then made a low, sorrowful moan and drove into the canal at the end of our street.

No one ever spoke about what we'd witnessed that morning. The Edelsteins moved out before the sun had had another chance to set. According to the grapevine, their granddaughter has never been found. Mort Gray, president of the neighborhood association, hired a private trash collection service the very next morning, and that was that.

On Silver Street, no one ever goes out after midnight these days. No matter what. Just over half the original homeowners have relocated or passed on since that summer. Before she died, Geraldine Rosenblum wrote to us that she never again saw a single duck swim in that canal. Shortly after the incident, Patrick and I purchased a double-wide mobile home and several acres of desert in Joshua Tree, California. It's a long way from the temperate Gulf Coast. There are few neighbors, mostly young blue-collar families. There are no lawns, no picket fences, and no paved road leading to our property. Most importantly, there's no trash collection.

#

Zombie revisionist, gadfly, and snake-oil merchant, MB Vigil is an East Coast native who reads Poe, and less blood-curdling literature, with at-risk students in the American Southwest. His evenings are spent at a neo-Gothic mahogany desk drafting, editing, and revising; poring over Gorey-illustrated classic horror anthologies—Lovecraft, Derleth, Aickman—in an oversized red velvet armchair, or perched at the foot of the bed mesmerized by Hitchcock and *Night Gallery* marathons on late-night nostalgia TV. As a result, he is always behind on grading papers

Pilot Holes

by Colton Adrian

You wouldn't think so, but even silence has a sound. Even underground, through torchlit tunnels and between concrete enforced walls you can hear it. Even when you get kidnapped and locked to a chair with enough chain to lasso a Georgia Pine, it comes from inside you, past your eardrums. Because even when an electric drill has spun both eardrums to a soft pulp and tiny rivers of blood trickle from each ear, even then, the silence is the loudest.

Why? Well, that doesn't matter but what your brain is trying to do is make up for the lack of stimuli. Or in this case, the destruction of any future indication of stimuli coming in through your mashed potato eardrums. It's the TV on in the background to make things less awkward. It's the fan that helps you fall asleep at night. It's a constant voice that's only talking to you every time you aren't listening. You try to loosen the chains but they get tighter, and the driller goes slower when you squirm.

Funny it seems, how suddenly eager to perceive information when balanced on the edge of death. Sad it seems, how life itself is less worth listening to than what follows it.

And I know it seems like this loud silence I'm talking about is just the whirl of the drill bouncing around your skull, but it isn't. When your crafty friend is switching out the battery from the drill you can still hear it. Try to make out the words, but you can't understand yet. Try to focus and the silence grows louder and more sporadic. You think maybe the sound is residue from being knocked unconscious prior to being slammed in a hollow trunk for transport. Maybe it's coming from the DMT being released from your pineal gland during this n(ear) death experience. Whatever the silent sound is, it can't be what I'm telling you it is because why haven't you heard it before? No way this is real anyway, right? Right on track with your Kübler-Ross, but you've lost too much blood to get angry enough for the next stage. You should have tried bargaining for a smaller drill bit an hour or two ago. You might have heard me sooner.

 I don't know how you're not dead yet. You look like a colander with all those pilot holes driven across your head. You stopped trying to loosen the chains a few holes ago. You can't hear anything but silence as each hole gets filled with a cobalt blue concrete screw. The twin lead threading on the screws themselves provide swift insertion into your brain at an angle for reduced settling torque.

 The idea is to get all the screws secure before you bleed out. The craftsman would like a moment or two of admiration for his work while you are still breathing. Each breath gets shorter as the sound of silence gets louder. His masterpiece is complete. Look how beautiful you are thirty feet underground, glistening sticky red. Marvelous, really.

 Now close your eyes. I need you to concentrate real hard so you can make out my voice. Look inside yourself and know me. Last chance. I've been here all along, but now you can finally understand what I've been saying. You are finally willing to listen.

Just when I'm all out of shit to say.

#

Colton Adrian is twenty-two. He plays with dirt at work and writes when he's not doing that. He escaped via C-section and was birthed in Williamsburg, Virginia. He's been there ever since and has been plotting a breakout involving a pen and a pad for the last two years. His work has appeared most recently in *The Molotov Cocktail* and *Leaves of Ink*.

Table

by Rhett Davis

Not too far from here, on the shore of a treeless island, what looks to be an enormous wooden table is partially buried in the sand. It has been there a long time. Centuries, the locals say, but would they really know? Generations distort the facts and water becomes wine. It's enough to say that the structure has been there for as long as people remember, stuck in the dunes, taller than the nearby buildings, waiting, it seems, for the return of its gargantuan chairs, their monstrous occupants and their bloody feasts.

No one knows what it is for sure. For a long time the islanders traded theories and far-fetched stories. It was said that the crew of a merchant vessel once sailed past a huge chair floating just under the waves, but when they turned back for a closer look it had gone. There was a rumour that a farmer had uncovered evidence of a forest on her pastures, seemingly cleared many years before people had arrived on the island. A group of fishermen once claimed they spied a vessel on the horizon so large it touched the bilious cumulonimbus. The vessel sped away with a pace that cannot be matched by any ship, car, or plane. But then, the islanders used to make grappa in their sheds. It was always very strong, and they used to make a lot of it.

Some said it was not a table at all. They suggested it might be the ruins of a dock built to transport immense cargoes by an ancient civilisation, or the remnants of an arcane defence against something prehistoric and terrible. Some declared it evidence of God; others that the structure was formed naturally over time by erosion. When pressed, these people admitted they were not scientists but insisted that did not make their opinion any less valid, demanding equal airtime in any television interviews. Archaeologists called it a monument; anthropologists a deity; botanists classified it as dead Quercus; and chemists a mix of carbon, oxygen, nitrogen, hydrogen and other trace elements. No one who has ever written a paper in a reputable scientific journal has ever called it a table—but that is what the islanders call it now. It was difficult to live next to something they couldn't name.

There used to be as much speculation about the nature of the alleged table and its origins as there were people on the island. But the islanders these days are the sort of people who have chosen to turn its legs into boutique seaside condominiums. They charge people to take pictures of it and climb it and jump from it with elastic cords attached to their ankles. They promote it in glossy brochures alongside expensive real estate and local wineries with their shabby pinot noir. They sell plastic souvenirs from market stalls and self-publish bullshit stories about the giants who used to roam the shores. They walk past it each day and pretend they don't stand in its heavy shadow. They don't speculate on its nature unless it's to make money. They have decided it is a table, and its name is now its truth. They have become the sort of people who look at something they do not understand and do not wonder about how strange and extraordinary it is but worry about how small it makes them feel. They are not the sort of people we should be listening to.

#

Rhett leaves quite often, but always comes back to Geelong, Australia. He has an MFA from the University of British Columbia in Vancouver, and has had fiction published in a number of journals in Australia and North America, including *The Sleepers Almanac*, *The Big Issue*, and *The Dalhousie Review*. He can be found at www.rhettdavis.com.

Bodies in the Snow

by Chris Milam

He slid to the mantel in his socked feet. On top sat a brushed-metal picture frame burdened with a glossy portrait of blonde chameleons wearing church clothes. Timmy cocked his head like a rifle, peeked in my direction with a blank, blue eye, but didn't act. He was a deliberate boy, a methodical half-man who understood that patience is a form of brutality.

I've been living in this festive dome for seven weeks. We arrived here in Michigan from a factory via the postal service; a family of three chasing the dream inside the curved walls of a seasonal trinket. It's just me now.

The boy's father was the first to break the pact, a couple of benign shakes a year didn't square with his greed for authority and domination. The image of his bleached, laughing teeth is a snuff film that loops in my mind from the night I lost my daughter, when he flicked his elegant hand and rolled us down the wood floors of the hallway like a bowling ball. Their three-legged cat, Roscoe, found the wreckage and licked the glass clean, as if he could have fixed anything with a kind tongue. While we grieved, safe and unbroken in a Victorian carriage, the father traded fist-bumps with his son. The family celebrated with a bucket of spicy-glazed chicken wings and iced cola. Ate pie for dessert.

The kid plopped down on the charcoal sectional, switched on a crime show, and went about mimicking a typical teenager. He took a sip of strawberry milk. Scratched his armpits. Cheered at the gunshots on the screen. His casual laziness was as comforting to me as a concrete pillow. I understood Timmy and I knew the score. He yawned. I waited.

His mother, a ponytailed menace with a taste for cream pantsuits, honed her own black cleaver in this suburban butcher shop. At night, she would approach our home on the oak slab, extend a French-manicured finger and roust us from a deep sleep with a rhythmic tapping.

Clink. Clink. Clink.

Polished madness.

Clink. Clink. Clink.

She was relentless and never tired. That pretty nail of hers tapping on the glass, the conductor of an insane melody that sought more than just our surrender. She wasn't the creator of torture, but she grasped its nuances, those pressure points that snapped one's resolve like a paper-thin cracker, erasing any doubt to who dictated the household law.

The rest of the family began to filter into the room, including Alexis, the one person in the house who I originally thought could play the savior. She always wore pink pajamas with faded rainbows on them, and drank hot cocoa with those tiny marshmallows drowning on top. Her crayon drawings of suns and trees hung on the burgundy walls. Once, she set us in front of the fireplace while she giggled at the exploits of Dora the Explorer and munched on candy corn. Her innocent smile curled wicked as the heat blistered our home, turning it into a cauldron of wintry funeral stew. The flame, like Alexis, did not believe in tender gestures. The hysteria that exploded from my wife's throat when she howled her final words is a sound that ruins a man. I failed her when I saved myself inside a red-wrapped artificial gift. Her screams continue to move under my skin, an accusation living in the noise of terror.

The father held me like a glass infant as the clan marched to the kitchen. Timmy grinned like a carved pumpkin when he opened the freezer. I glanced back into the living room, at the aquarium, where a lone striped fish stared back at me with a sympathetic, dazed eye. He seemed to know the score, too. When the door slammed shut, nightfall came in a flash. I could have pleaded with them to spare me, tapped out a SOS, retreated to my plastic home, but there are times when you must accept your fate. And your cowardice. They had pled allegiance to hate long before we arrived in a cardboard box, and to try and reason or negotiate with a dark pulse seemed pointless. My family was as dispensable to them as a used coffee filter.

As the glass began to frost, I scooped up a handful of fake snow, tossed it high into the air. The white flakes floating above were as pristine and haunting as Timmy's unblemished pale face.

#

Chris Milam lives in the bucolic wasteland that is Hamilton, Ohio. When not writing, he vapes and sulks with ferocity. His stories have appeared in *The Airgonaut, WhiskeyPaper, Jellyfish Review, Bartleby Snopes,* and elsewhere.

A Hands-Off Approach

by Sherry Morris

The hand had been with her as far back as she could remember. As a small child, it would poke out of the kitchen bin, shaking its forefinger in displeasure when she tried to throw away gifts she'd received from him. When she started school, it appeared as a *Stop!* in front of the girls' loos. He had convinced her mother that public restrooms were a haven of germs and perverts—that only the house bathroom was safe. But she knew there was no safety from the watchful eyes that peered at her through doors cracks, and the hands that patiently waited for the right time to act. She had no vocabulary to describe these activities to her mother, so she said nothing. As she got older, the hand would appear in the mirror in a thumbs-down gesture as she readied herself for school, reinforcing his idea that no one else would want her. When she hit puberty the hand would scratch at her budding breasts as she dried herself after bathing. Scratch and scratch and scratch at the warm, tender skin, leaving large, red welts that turned to small, white scars. As a teenager, when she imagined telling someone about the hand, it would leap to her throat, squeezing tight around her neck till thoughts of speaking out left her entirely. Eventually she moved out and the hand left her alone. For a while. But then she had to go for crisis care. They wanted her to talk about herself while lying on a sofa. She did and discovered the hand resting lightly on her chest, just below her neck, tapping softly—a gentle reminder it was still there. That it was still important to keep quiet. They didn't seem to notice it. She didn't mention it and hoped it would leave her in peace. She hadn't learned.

The hand decided to stick around and make up for lost time. While riding the bus, she watched it try to pinch schoolgirls' bottoms. Sometimes it laid innocently on an empty seat, waiting for women to accidentally sit on it. Then it began tormenting her. Pulling her hair. Or rather, pulling out her hair. There were other things the hand did to her. To other parts of her. With objects. The day it poured boiling water on her genitals she knew she had to do something.

She has done her research and prepared carefully. She has chosen the ladies' restroom of the public library. A notice states guns are not allowed in the library; this does not concern her, she intends to use an axe. She has spent weeks strengthening her left hand and learning to use it. Practicing on cuts of meat and bone bought from the butcher till her aim is perfect and she can chop straight through with one stroke. She's brought bandages for after and a flask of whisky for before. She needs to work quickly lest she be interrupted—either by a person or the hand. She takes a long swig from the flask, then looks at herself in the mirror and nods. It is time. She lays her right arm on the marble counter between two sinks. It is cold. She keeps the main part of her mind distracted while quietly focusing. She has learned how to dissociate. She picks up the axe in her left hand and brings it swiftly down on her right wrist. Through searing pain she feels joyous relief. Blood spatters on the mirror, her blouse, and it begins to pool in the sink. In spite of the pain she smiles. It is a clean chop. The hand twitches in front of her. Working quickly, she wraps the stump in bandages. Then throws the hand in the toilet and flushes. She doesn't want it to be found. She walks out of the ladies and approaches the check-out desk, holding her bloody stump. The librarian begins to scream. *Shh, shh,* she scolds. *This is a library.* And then she faints. Afterwards, she refuses any type of prosthetic, insisting she will manage fine. The first six months are bliss. There is the occasional pain in her phantom hand, but she's read that's normal. Then one morning she wakes with her left hand gently resting around her neck. She thinks it's a coincidence 'til it happens three nights in a row. Then she notices it tracing the scars on her chest as she dries herself after bathing, the fingers flexing as if preparing to dig in. She will take no chances.

She begins strengthening her toes.

#

Sherry grew up in Missouri and now lives in London, writing short stories while dreaming of early retirement. She grows elephant garlic, eats crumpets, and drinks hot tea with milk—though not simultaneously. Her work can be found at www.uksherka.com and she sometimes tweets from @Uksherka.

Phenomena

House Spiders

by Shane Page

    We walk together in the dark. I am awake. Sometimes porch lights turn off and on. Sometimes little bats fly by. Sometimes spiders with wiggly legs tap dance on people's porches, and their arms are humanoid but cartoon, and their hats are straw with red ribbons. I feel their beady eyes follow us. They wait for our backs to turn.
    The yards are full of spiders, big spiders, living a nightlife somewhere between vaudeville and Alabamian roadside circus. Spiders on skateboards, bikes, rollerblades, unicycles. Spiders socializing and smoking, sharing weird talents and cocktail party knowledge. They are as tall as me. My dog, Samwise, and I keep walking. Samwise's stethoscope hangs from his collar and scrapes on the sidewalk; his head mirror lights our way.
    Here is how we walk:
    I found this yellow radio you could attach to your belt if you wanted, so I did. It has a headphone jack, but the only compatible headphones are these huge gray ones that look like anti-tank landmines with a curly cord. It also has a flashlight

built in. It's burnt out. The radio hangs from me, big as a toolbox, its cord reaching up to the twin pans on my head, making my shadow look like something alien.

Samwise's short legs click, *tictactictac*. He is half Scottie, half Schnauzer, and has black fur. His collar has skulls on it. He is small and fat. He sounds like Louis Armstrong.

"Do you think they want to eat us?" I ask him, as he walks in front of me without a leash and looks both ways before crossing the street. A spider with no special skill skitters in front of us. It is not lifting two-ton weights or dancing the can-can or juggling bowling pins.

"I think some of them want to eat us," Samwise says as a spider bigger than a kitchen table scurries up a tree. "I think others just want to have a good time."

The worst thing about the neighborhood spiders is how quiet they are. Here they are on everyone's porches: drinking, dancing, singing. Everything they do is as loud as a whisper. They are only here for an hour each night. If you listen closely you can hear the ones in the trees spinning their webs.

*

I knew I was in for some trouble when I started seeing spiders in my bed. Not little house spiders scrambling across my sheets to find a new dark corner. These were tarantulic beasts, thick legs, fuzzy black bodies, walking with careful steps as if trying not to wake me, each appendage folding out and back to edge closer and closer to me like a rickety, obsidian eight-fingered hand.

They weren't real. It was only after they'd melted into my blankets that I became afraid. A hypnagogic hallucination, a vision associated with sleep paralysis. Some people see spiders floating in the air or playing violin or driving little cars, others see spiders inches away from their eyes on a pillow. Some people've got beds full of snakes, demons on their chest, dead relatives gathered at the foot of their bed, watching, bluish, malicious.

The thing about sleep paralysis is you accept everything like an idiot. The horror comes seconds later. And I think back, realize the thorax of the spider wasn't a solid body, but overlapping lines of Sharpie scribbles, a tornado of ink. And the legs were sewn-together miniature cotton balls. Maybe they only wanted to crawl by and say hello before melting away. The slow, relaxed tarantulas, walking and melting, walking and melting.

So when breathing exercises and sleeping pills didn't do much, I started taking old Samwise for nighttime walks, and we met our nighttime neighbors.

*

"Are you tired?" I ask Samwise as we pass a group of kid spiders throwing rocks at a stack of milk bottles. The adult spider next to the bottles whispers, "Knock 'em down, win a prize. Knock 'em down for a jar of flies."

"No. Are you?" Samwise looks back at me, and the light from his head mirror is blinding.

"No."

"You have to sleep sometime."

He's right. He is a good doctor.

When the sun starts to rise, the spiders scamper away. They lift sidewalk slabs and burrow underneath, crawl into small attic windows. They untie their skates, kiss goodbye, and carry large, webbed sacks of collected bugs on which they will dine.

A spider up ahead cleans up his yard sale. Everything Must Go, his sign says, Prices Negotiable. He is not like the others with their hats and ties and corn cob pipes. He is just a black spider, the size of a PT Cruiser.

While we pass, he says, "Want anything? I need some money." His voice sounds like a Hollywood demon. He looks at me with eyes like green olives packed into vats of vinegar. His chelicerae glisten in Samwise's light. Samwise mumbles, "Just keep walking."

But the salesman is desperate, and he springs over his wares and blocks the sidewalk. He begs, front legs mocking how humans beg, pleading with us to buy something. He's got kids, thousands. We try to pass, but he always runs ahead of us. I hate the way his legs sound on the ground. Thick, soft taps.

He implores, he needs this. Samwise, though he is thirteen years old, assumes an offensive stance to protect us. The spider spreads his eight legs wide and snaps his fangs together. Syrupy venom oozes to the ground. The sun is rising and the grass is slowly changing from blue to green. I flip on the radio on my belt. It cycles through morning shows. *Good morning, rock fans. Before we get to the news. Before we get to the next song. There's a traffic jam on I-55.* Little spider children round up their toys and climb into trees. One of them drops his baseball. "I'm sorry," I say to the spider. "I've really gotta get home."

#

Shane lives in Springfield, Missouri. He is an undergraduate student at Missouri State University where he studies professional and creative writing.

Season of the Dead

by Robin Jeffrey

When the snow first came, the inhabitants of the little village were joyous. It had been a dry spring and a hard, long summer, and the crops had failed and the animals had died standing in the dusty fields and the villagers had been forced to trade away their valuables to the towns on the other side of the mountains for any water at all.

Many had been praying that the winter would bring snow; good, wet ice that would seep into the ground and keep their fields green through the growing and harvesting times. They had received, seemingly in abundance, that for which they prayed. The wind brushed the white tufts into arcing banks against the cottages and shops and many a celebratory pint of ale was had in the tavern the night of the first snow.

There was some debate amongst the older men of the village if there truly was a first snow and a second snow. Some swore that the first storm must have stopped in the night, sometime on the third or fourth day. Other's contended that, though it made no sense, the snow had never stopped after that first night, despite the fact that the frozen rain was still falling steadily nearly a fortnight later.

At first, villagers had tried to shovel paths from their doors to the roads to their barns and to their neighbors. Each morning a figure could be seen outside each house, pushing a spade heaped high with snow, tossing their pile atop the previous-days' work. But soon, the banks of snow were too high and the falling snow too think and steady for anyone to deal with, and the villagers retreated into their homes, muttering with waning cheerfulness about how much the snowfall was needed and how it wouldn't last much longer because nothing could last forever.

The snow engulfed the barns and the houses and the shops and the pub. It buried the fields under feet and feet of white ice, choking the youngest saplings that stood around the village until the tops of their bare branches barely broke through the surface of the new, white ground. Suffocating, not a sound could be heard in the village, not the tinkling of icicles or the heavy breathing of sleeping cattle or the soft moans of the villagers praying that the snow would stop as fervently as they had prayed it would come.

When spring finally came, it was with all the warmth and beauty of a young girl entering her first dance. Sun broke through the grey clouds of winter with a flash and all the cold barrenness of the season prior was hard to imagine.

The towns on the other side of the mountains began to worry about the little village after the third week of the thaw. The passes had been cleared for some time and it seemed strange that none of their neighbors had come to trade or barter, to partake in the first of the spring ale or size up the big sow's new parcel of offspring.

A party of men were sent over the mountain to check on the small village. Disease, rampant illnesses that tore through men and animals alike, were not unheard of in that time and it was worried that such a fate had befallen the little village in the freezing winter months, when no aid could be called for or sent.

A week or so later the men returned. To this day none of them talk about what they saw in the place where the little village once was. The mention of winter makes them shiver even on the hottest days of summer, and the season itself is met with fear quite unusual for such men of the earth to display. A few pints of ale will loosen some of their tongues, loosen them enough to make them whisper, in hoarse tones, of the sodden marshland that stood where the little village had been. Of the structures, vanished, and the sounds of ice dripping, dripping even though none could be seen. The winter had claimed the little village and every living thing in it. None ventured there again, but it was said that in the cruel, cold winds that came over the mountains, the wails of the men and women and children of the village still echoed, immortal and dead as the winter itself.

#

Robin Jeffrey was born in Cheyenne, Wyoming to a psychologist and a librarian, giving her a love of literature and a consuming interest in the inner workings of people's minds, passions which have served her well as she pursues a career in creative writing. Currently, Robin lives in Klamath Falls, Oregon, where she enjoys exercising her brain as the Library Director at Klamath Community College, spending time with her husband Phil, and playing with their Siborgi, Leo.

Dream Logic

by R.A. Roth

Two rules you must always obey.
Never dream. Never disturb my slumber.
Or face oblivion. – J. the Dreaming God

    J. dreamt that he was a god who, in order to maintain his power, inhibited the public's will to dream. It wasn't impossible to dream. Just perilous. Doctors couldn't figure out what had squelched the desire to dream, so J., as a benevolent god, went on all manner of social media and TV to tell the public that he, their new god, was the party responsible for poisoning the dream well.
    "I apologize for the inconvenience," J. said, nearing the conclusion of his apology, which ended with a fair exchange.
    "As recompense for lost dreams, I bequeath the ability to stay awake indefinitely, fully alert and well. Bless you all," he said, and all of social media and TV reverted to its normal traffic flow.
    In the days that followed, the world underwent some drastic changes. Sleep-related industries collapsed. Businesses unaffected by the death of sleep switched to around-the-clock

operations. An extra meal, midmunch, was added to the daily regimen. Food consumption skyrocketed 40%, so the US government ceased paying farmers to not grow basic staples such as corn, soybeans and wheat. The workday was lengthened to 12 hours, with a corresponding increase in pay, and the economy boomed. In less than a fortnight, the Dow soared over 30,000 and so fattened the pockets of a few opportunistic speculators that they quit their jobs and retired to lives of 24-hour luxury. The luckiest of the speculators was Dr. Monist Albums, a SoCal OB/GYN who lived in a 35-room palace overlooking copy-and-paste McMansions, boxy condos and assorted commercial developments. Dr. Albums invested heavily in electronics and game console makers, betting those surplus hours were more likely to get gobbled up on leisure activities, and he turned a mere fortune into a mega-fortune. Monist's wife of seven years celebrated by making an appointment to have her currently generous helping of boobs inflated to the size of dirigibles. J. oversaw the operation himself.

"Relax, Mrs. Albums," he said, "you won't feel a thing." But when the anesthesiologist tried to put Mrs. Albums under, nothing happened. Sleep, including artificially-induced sleep, had been eradicated. Her case was far from unusual or isolated. Unable to anesthetize patients, surgeons around the world were forced to perform dangerous, intricate procedures on conscious subjects, the majority of whom lapsed into shock and died.

In response to a public health crisis, J. issued a new edict: "I return to the world the ability to sleep dreamlessly. To compensate for lost dreams, I bequeath the power to read minds. Bless you all."

With sleep back on the table, the sleep industry experienced an instant rebirth, as one would expect. The mass introduction of mind-reading, however, didn't go over as smoothly. In less than a fortnight the divorce rate quadrupled. Families who survived the sudden influx of naked secrets ate their meals in solitude and blasted music to drown out the torrential cloudbursts of unabated thoughts infiltrating their heads. Young men, biologically preoccupied with sexual congress and the female figure, tried squelching their unchecked fantasies by mentally reciting times tables, passages from books, hypnotic mantras, and even then brash involuntary declarations of sexual enticement, *I want to fuck that girl so badly, will I ever touch a pussy, a nipple?* escaped into the unprotected wilderness of human thought. High school teachers went on strike citing mind-reading as an untenable distraction which made it impossible to conduct an orderly class. Public events were canceled. Worldwide, every stripe of politician chose the life of a hermit or was imprisoned by the state, including but not limited to the President of the United States, Martin Mendass, whose head was a minefield of sensitive state secrets, nuclear launch codes and political intrigues. On the plus side of the ledger, business meetings were discarded for actual productive work.

A week into the mind-reading debacle, J. usurped mass communication channels for a third time to address the world: "I return to the world the ability to think privately, with no change in the policy of dreamless sleep. As fair compensation for lost dreams, I bequeath a universal IQ of 200. Bless you all."

Supercharging humanity's brainpower jumpstarted an unprecedented worldwide pursuit of knowledge. In less than a fortnight, incredible theories were discovered and refined, and the least controversial of these theories proved beyond all doubt that the creation of the universe and subsequent evolutionary processes were godless enterprises. In response, the coalition of minds responsible for the godless universe theory drafted and published a scathing column lambasting J. for his godly pretense. They called him a fraud, a charlatan, a snake oil salesmen preying on the gullible. Head of the coalition, Pope Morpheus, declared that J. was a shockingly unscrupulous phony beyond forgiveness.

"You're all making a terrible mistake," J. said on his J.Tube channel. "As your god, if you turn your backs on me, I shall slumber no more and upon awakening end the world and all of you."

The world challenged J.'s assertion, deemed outrageous and beyond the pale of logic and reason, and turn its back on him. The sudden loss of worshipers woke J. up, and upon waking J. heard the dwindling screams of ten billion souls pleading for mercy as the world faded to black.

"I had the strangest dream," J. told his wife, K. the Dreaming God, and she banished him to the cold wasteland of space for trying to steal her powers.

#

In addition to *The Molotov Cocktail*, R.A. Roth's work has appeared at *Noble / Gas Qtrly*, *Chicago Literati*, and *Helen: A Literary Magazine*. His novella, *Tetraminion*, was recently released. He tweets about this and that under the handle @fantagor.

The Summer of Infinite Possibilities

by G.G. Silverman

You rushed in the back door that afternoon, slamming dog-eared books on the table while blurting your carnival-going plans to Mother. She looked up, eyeing you cold over the butcher block, her hardened face a warning. Sweat-damp hair hung limp as she sliced beets rhythmically, their blood tainting her fingers, her knife thudding the block. She said nothing, only wiped her hands on a grimy apron where Rorschach patterns bloomed.

You became silent, wishing you could spool your plans back into your mouth, and wind them down, down, down into the dark safe place in your heart. You didn't tell Mother you and Will were headed there anyway; you'd dump out your jam jar and see what those dirty nickels bought you. Then you'd both ride down on your bikes, grinning stupid for the last day of school and the beginning of your summer adventures. This would be your summer of finding yourself, your Summer of Getting Lost.

You ditched your bikes in the weeds by the rusted fence that separated the fairgrounds from the town, and its wilting, faded-paint normalcy. A dusty-suited, buck-toothed man guarded the gate, fingering a greasy roll of tickets. You turned out your pockets, trading your lint and change for entrance. The man wiped his brow with his jacket-sleeve and tore off a section of the roll. His hand touched yours for the slightest of moments and it felt cold, waxy. You pulled away and mumbled thanks, darting after your best friend, already on his way to the fun house. Another man stood outside the fun house with glassy eyes; droplets studded his bulbous, near-bald head. With no soul in his voice, he asked for your tickets and you gave them willingly. His hand, too, was cold.

Will darted in first, hollering in the passageway, and you followed, though Will was already gone, made invisible by the maze. You could see yourself on all sides, mirrored infinitely into space until you presumably reached the ends of the Earth. You felt lost and found all at once, not knowing which of yourselves was true, yet knowing more about yourself than you ever had. You had the detached eye of a god, seeing yourself through time.

But you were alone.

You resumed looking for passage, but kept hitting mirrored walls. You groped to find your way out. You couldn't hear Will anymore, and called his name.

I'm almost out, he said, his voice sounding far.

Your upper lip felt damp. *Okay*, you said, *Okay. I'll be there soon.*

You fumbled past more mirrors, breath becoming short, walls closing in, until you were sure you were almost there. But you still didn't know how to get out. You could only see a reflection of the exit, and in that reflection, you saw Will outside. You called his name again, and he called back, and you saw one of your infinite selves follow.

Let's go home, you heard him say to Will outside. Let's go home.

\#

G.G. Silverman lives north of Seattle with her husband and dog. She is the author of *Vegan Teenage Zombie Huntress*, a comedic feminist YA zombie novel that was also a finalist for the North Street Book Prize. G.G's short fiction has won awards and her work has been featured in Pop Seagull's *Robotica* anthology, *Deathlehem Revisited* by Grinning Skull Press, Pulp Modern's *Dangerous Women* (writing pseudonymously as Janna Darkovich), *Iconoclast* magazine, and more. To connect with G.G., please visit her site at www.ggsilverman.com.

Waiting

by Jan Kaneen

The reflection is always on tenterhooks, waiting, nervously behind the silvery dividing line, in the slipstream reaches of the netherworld, waiting for him to pass.

Like all reflections, it must be quicksilver to appear at precisely the right time in exactly the right place, perfectly shape-shifted.

Bathroom mirrors are not much of a challenge, being regular, frequent and painless, but they are the exception, not the rule.

Shop windows every day, on the way through the city are trickier, more transient and unpredictable.

The windows on packed tubes demand more skill and total concentration. The reflection must one moment be transparent and ghostly against daytime glass and then instantly solid and full-colored against underground, obsidian black.

Rainy day panes on the train to and from Waterloo are torture. They require the reflection to undergo sustained fragmentation, which is both demanding and excruciating, like being ripped to pieces and dislocated innumerable times, pulled apart into agonized smithereens.

The potbellied, brass coal-bucket on the hearth at home and the forks at dinner are painful as you can imagine. The millpond at midnight when the water is as still as mirrors is an unexpected surprise.

They've never been here before.

He's holding a counterpart bottle of scotch, half-drunk as the reflection looks up and sideways, trying to catch the words being uttered from beyond. It's hard for the reflection to hear because it's doubling itself, appearing at once flat and perfect in the water and shrunken and distorted in the bottle. The words are muffed and slurred, but it gets the gist.

Closing in, can't carry on, nothing to live for.

The reflection swallows too. Is this really happening? What are the chances? That a human being might kill themselves looking deep into their unbroken, perfect reflection, allowing one of them to escape and take his place? Almost no one abandons their body, gazing calm at their own still-reflected selves, which is why that is the rule; the cruel hopeful commandment that chains reflections like shadows to their masters.

Other reflections sense the potential and do the unthinkable, clamoring in excitedly at the impossibility, pushing like poltergeists just below the surface. Inanimate reflections, of trees, grass, cottages, the clear black sky, the moon and stars move in, closer, entranced, poised.

He doesn't notice. He's somewhere else, looking inside himself, so the pond and the reflections and the sky, and the trees and the universe don't exist, which is a shame because they're all right there, crowded in, in one still, small mill pond right before his eyes.

The reflection jostles away all the other reflections. This is its chance not theirs. But he's turned back, away from the brink, which tomorrow will be choppy ripples. If he dies here tomorrow the reflection must fragment like the pieces of a kaleidoscope, the chance shattered.

It would scream if it could, long and hard like a Siren or the Banshee it longs to be, but it's condemned to silence as well as everything else so it pulls itself together and goes to wait in the shadows by the bedroom window for him to draw the curtains.

The reflection is always on tenterhooks, waiting, hungrily, millimeters away, just behind the silvery dividing line in the close-by reaches of the netherworld, waiting for him to pass.

#

Jan Kaneen is a mum, wife, sister and full-time pug servant. In her spare time she fills it up. Her surname is KANEEN definitely *not* KEENAN— not that she has anything against the lovely Keenans from the island of Island, but her family is from the Isle of Man—a teeny weeny rock in the Irish sea between the island of Island and Liverpool. It's a Manx name— unusual and easy to get wrong but MANX nevertheless. Glad we got that sorted.

Wisdom Tooth

by Leanne Radojkovich

Celia woke as a crow flew at her. She covered her face just as it dissolved above her head.

That was the third crow to fly out of the bedroom wall. It scared her more than any other nightmare.

What if she ended up like her mother, who'd slept on the sofa with the lights on all night? Then stayed there for days with a teatowel across her eyes? Celia had had to tiptoe around making school lunches from crackers.

There'd been machine guns and snow in her mother's past. Celia had never seen a machine gun, or snow, and her mother hadn't seen a bikini until she was war-orphaned and shipped halfway across the planet.

Celia's ears filled with static: why couldn't her mother have enjoyed the present before it was too late?

She sat up and felt the air prickle.

A pair of little old people stepped out of the wall. The woman wore a black kerchief, the man a black shawl.

Celia blinked hard. They disappeared.

She went to work and tried not to think about the old couple and the crows.

The next day she woke and the air prickled again.

The old people stood close. "Don't you recognize us? We're your grandparents."

The little woman did resemble Celia's mother—if she'd worn a kerchief.

"We need a bone, small bone, fingertip, toe."

"Hurry, hurry," the old man shooed Celia into action. Did they want one of her toes?

Then a crow landed on the sill beside her mother's urn.

The little old couple rummaged inside until the woman pulled out a gravelly piece of ash—a tooth?

They waved to Celia and disappeared.

Celia waved back.

Had she gone mad?

She sank down on the bed.

The air softened.

A glimpse of cypresses and snow.

#

Leanne Radojkovich was born in New Zealand and lives in Auckland. Her stories have been widely published online and in print, and have won or been commended in various competitions including Ireland's Fish Short Story Prize and the National Flash Fiction Day NZ contest. She also posts flash fiction street art, which has appeared in unexpected places around the world from China to Sweden to Tanzania. www.leanneradojkovich.com.

The Cave

by Premee Mohamed

The woods are watching me. Or no, let me clarify—I don't mean 'the woods,' singular plural, consisting of trees, dirt, sky, and moss. Not exactly. I mean the things in the woods, the animals, or maybe just one thing, one animal, something with eyes…I'm sorry. Let me start over.

The woods started watching me when Cavanaugh disappeared.

The invite was made last year, at his tiny cabin tucked between the creek and the trees, juggling venison steaks on the grill: "Ben, come with me next year. Don't waste the drive; whatever we shoot, we'll split. " And so, be-tagged, be-gunned, in my safety orange, I came on Monday. A perfect autumn day—clear and still with golden leaves hanging on the aspens like coins, a skiff of frost on the mud. I hadn't been hunting since I was a kid, but it stays with you. Cav laughed when I said so. "It does," he said. "Look how quiet you're putting your feet down. We'll have a freezer full of eats in an hour."

But it was five hours before we saw our first buck, meaty and sleek with a dainty six-point rack. Cav semaphored with blinks: his shot. I squatted in silence while he set up. A crack, a crash; the buck flung himself through the brush as I ran to look for sign on the frozen ground. "Did you get him? I don't see any blood."

"Sometimes the hit plugs the flow for a minute. Let's track. Brother's got barbecue written all over him."

A thing in pain will rush downhill, seeking to save energy and blood, trying to get a lead on its enemy; but the traces we found of the buck went up, till finally the trees got stunted and mean, the leaves no longer gold but gray. It was Cavanaugh who found the cave; we stopped in the entrance, catching our breath.

"He never went in there," I said.

"Animals do funny things when they're hurt," he insisted, fumbling for his lighter. The tiny, shivering light illuminated a few feet of black stone walls, a stone floor paved with leaves. Were they disturbed, had a path been made? I couldn't tell. It smelled like animal though—unwashed, rank, sweaty fur and sour secretions. A warm, odorous breeze fought with Cav's lighter.

"No deer would—" I began, then saw something in the fading flame. I picked it up, sure that it was bone, but no—a piece of chalk. Just ordinary, schoolroom chalk, half worn down. I weighed it in my hand, then tossed it off the edge.

"Weird."

"Yeah—ow!" Cav brought his hand to his mouth, sucked, spat red into the cave. "Jesus. Cut myself on the rock. Let's go. Damn bad luck."

We trudged downwards, hanging onto the saplings at either side of the path, funny how uphill becomes easier than downhill as your knees start to go. "How you doing, you old bastard?" I said, and turned to see the empty path.

May I never forget the pure sharpness, the clarity, of that moment of panic. "Cav?" Beating the bushes, calling, scaring birds out of the trees. And knowing, somehow, that he was gone—hadn't slipped off the trail and fallen to his death, hadn't gotten ahead of me to the truck. Was just gone. I returned in silence, throat raw from yelling. Texted, called: nothing. Finally there seemed to be an answer, but it was just a click and then the chuckle of running water. I thought: The worst, the worst has happened.

Yeah, I called the local police. They asked the usual: name, age, description. And then, very strangely: "Well, we'll send search and rescue, but I gotta tell you, sir, we'd be more likely to get out there for a kid or whatnot. Y'know. Takes a little while to organize. A forty-eight-year-old guy with some woodcraft, he'll be fine. The woods'll look after him. You'll see."

And since then I've been in the cabin, nape prickling, intensely watched, as raw as a nerve. I called Alece to say I loved her. "Ben, you silly creature," she laughed. "You could have just texted. How's Cav doing? Send him my love! You boys shoot something real big, OK?"

At least I did that. A small comfort. Afterwards, I bolted the wooden shutters and drew the blackout curtains, and I've been hiding here in front of the fire ever since. But of course the problem with blocking the windows so nothing can see in is that I can no longer see out, and so I can't tell, exactly, what is making that scritching noise outside, that cozy, creaturely, third-grade noise, of someone or something scribbling with chalk on the wall of the cabin, the one that faces into the woods.

#

Premee Mohamed is a scientist and spec fic writer working out of Canada. In her spare time she likes to annotate her copy of the *Necronomicon* in case she's missed anything.

A Man of Many Hats

by Aeryn Rudel

I tell people I'm a man of many hats. Most think that means I'm a man of many talents. That's also true, but I do wear a lot of hats, and each one makes me something different.

Right now, as I cross the street following the blond man, I'm wearing a baseball cap. There's a logo on the front: a stylized D. I don't know which team that represents; I'm not a sports fan. What I do know is that my eyesight is much better than usual, and my right arm feels like it's made of stronger stuff than flesh and bone, like iron or steel. I have Superman's arm.

The baseball cap arrived in the same package as the other hats, appearing on my doorstep this morning at 8 a.m., just like always. I heard the thump as it hit my doormat, but, as usual, no one was there when I opened the door. Inside the package were three hats: the baseball cap, a camouflage army cap, and a white cloth headband with a Japanese symbol on it. There was also a heavy round stone, a pistol, and a picture of the blond man with an address and a time printed (not handwritten) on the reverse. The baseball cap had a sticky note attached to it. Written on the note in black Sharpie was the number 1.

I hadn't known what any of this was for, the hats or the other things. That would come later. I had put the baseball cap on my head, put the rest in my bag, then headed downtown. I went to the address on the back of the picture at the right time and waited for the blond man to arrive. He did. Just like I knew he would. The addresses and times are always right.

I've been following the blonde man for ten minutes. He doesn't know I'm behind him. If he did, he wouldn't walk away from the more populated center of town, under the bridge where it's dark and no one can see us. He's got a briefcase, and he's dressed nice, like a businessman: crisp white shirt, black slacks and sports coat. Maybe they want what's in the case. I never really know what it is they want, or even who they are. I don't need to; I like our arrangement. They send the hats and the other things, and when I'm done, they send money, a lot of money. The closet it is nearly filled with stacks of bills. I should buy something soon.

The blond man has stopped and turned around, and he sees me. He also sees he is alone and in a place where no one can help him. His eyes are wide and frightened. Sometimes the people know I'm there to hurt them; other times they seem completely surprised. The blonde man knows, and he turns to run.

Now I know what the baseball cap is for. Now I know what the round stone is for. Images and words flood into my head. Words like four-seam grip, windup, come set, and kick and throw. On the top level of my mind, I don't understand these words, but the primitive brain, the part that controls my body, understand them perfectly. My fingers close around the stone in a precise grip, and I bring my hands together at my waist, rock back on my left foot, then step and throw the stone as hard as I can. My arm feels good and strong as I throw the stone, and from over sixty feet away, it strikes the blond man in the back of the head with a hollow THWOK! He falls to the ground.

I start forward, digging in my bag for the next hat. I come up with the headband. I flip the baseball cap off my head and put the headband on. Now I feel quick, nimble, and I really want to hit something, or better yet, kick something.

I rush forward as the blond man is getting to his feet. He has a pistol in his hand, and there is blood on the collar of his white shirt. He aims the pistol at me. Again, information slams into my brain and my body responds. My right hand shoots out and catches the blond man's wrist. I marvel at my own speed and precision. I twist the blonde man's wrist back at a precise angle, and he gasps in pain and drops the gun. Still holding him, I lash out in a short powerful kick at the blond man's knee. The knee snaps, bending the wrong way, and he screams. I let go of his wrist, and he falls to the ground.

It is time for the last hat. I take off the headband, pull the camouflage cap from the bag, and set it on my head. Now I want the gun. I need the gun. I take the pistol from the bag, and I know everything about it. I hear words like Sig Sauer and .45 ACP and headshot.

The blond man holds up his hands and says something in a language I don't understand. They didn't give me a hat for that. I point the gun at his head and he opens his mouth, maybe to scream for help. I pull the trigger. The gun bucks in my hand and unleashes a tremendous sound. I shoot the blond man in his open mouth, and the gray sidewalk behind him is splashed with red. He collapses and dies.

I take off the camouflage hat and put it and the gun back in the bag. I put the bag on the blond man's body. Tomorrow, the body will be gone, there will be no mention of his death in the news, and the bag will be on my back porch filled with money. It's time to go home. I'm out of hats.

#

Aeryn Rudel is a freelance writer from Seattle, Washington. He is a notorious dinosaur nerd, a rare polearms expert, a baseball connoisseur, and he has mastered the art of fighting with sword-shaped objects (but not actual swords). Aeryn's first novel, *Flashpoint*, was recently published by Privateer Press, and he occasionally offers dubious advice on the subjects of writing and rejection (mostly rejection) on his blog at www.rejectomancy.com.

Aria

by Seth Augenstein

The figures invaded my home. They touched things. Their dirty fingers clawed the smooth dust on my mantel and my candelabra. A few of the biddies rifled through the dresses in my closet. A kid picked his nose and wiped it on the plush chair at the head of the dining room table. They smelled. I could feel their wheezing breaths, their heavy footsteps straining my floorboards. They swept through the house like those Hessians my great-great grandmother still babbles about from her place in the attic.

The wind whipped a light rain against the east windows. A moonless October night. They whispered to one another in the dark corners, thinking no one would hear. I heard. I whispered to them.

"You hear that?" one said.

"No. Ghosts don't exist," said the other.

A familiar shape led them. Lance carried a candle at the front, just as he did every October. Lance, that charlatan, led them from the side entrance to the pantry, through the servants' stairwell, and up to the bedrooms. He told them about intrigues and crimes unsolved within these walls, other nonsense stories.

The horde inspected Jacob's favorite chair, the corner where we held hands after we'd lost Nathan. The shadows where Sarah cried as a girl.

Lance had gained even more weight, his steps were heavier on the floorboards. His fat neck jiggled, sending sweat and spit flying as his voice electrified the intruders.

"Tell me what you feel," he said. "Tell me if you feel a presence, something cold or warm, close or far."

The biddies, clad in black, heavy makeup and momentous crosses looped around spindly necks, touched their chests and gasped. They pointed way over to the darkest corner, mouths hung open.

"It's there," one of them said. "A male presence, something evil."

I stood over her shoulder, shaking my head. Then I drifted behind Lance, who had his arms folded, one finger at his lip.

"Yes, I'm sensing that, too," he said.

I pinched his ass. But he couldn't sense that.

None of them ever heard or felt me. These sensitive souls were simply the best impostors.

I did not number among them. In life, I was a pragmatic woman, running a household for a demanding man, five children, and ne'er-do-well cousins and uncles. Throughout my days there was always something to fix, something to scrub or fold, a visitor at the door, or a crying child. In all my 74 years, these things occupied moment after moment, for a lifetime.

The Reverend at church never said anything about my eternal reward being more of the same. Sure, I have my solitude in the spring and winter and summer. But my peace is broken every autumn by crowds kicking up dust, taking out my china, as Lance waits at the front door of my house with a wicker basket, charging these idiots admission.

This year I had plans, however.

As the herd continued through the dining room, leaving their dirt and stink everywhere, I moved between them, among them to the parlor. I tickled their necks, I pulled at their shoelaces. The wide window shows the stormy sky, and the dead trees on the lawn. The wallpaper here is dramatic. It was always my favorite room. Of course Lance held the sham séance here every year.

I positioned myself at the back. The gawkers sat in row after row facing Lance, who reclined on the loveseat, elbow propped theatrically on the armrest.

The séance began. Lance instructed them to hold hands, and I felt their hearts beat faster. They sweat and stink. Lance's act is comical: all beseeching, imploring and commanding. I snorted.

At this one little boy raised his head. It was the nosepicker. He turned to me. I gasped. The first intuitive among the hundreds to come through my door. Looking into that young shadow-crossed face, inspiration struck me.

"Anyone feel anything?" said Lance.

The boy raised a hand.

"The lady tells me you're a fraud."

Lance sat bolt upright.

"What did you say?"

"I didn't say it. The lady told me. She said, 'You're a fraud, Lance.'"

Lance breathes, deep and slow.

"She wants you to know," the boy said, "you're full of shit."

The crowd hushed. The boy's mother smacked his arm. The biddies in black and crosses gasped, hands at their throats.

"That must be the old crone, an unclean spirit…"

"She says you've gotten fat. You stink. She says you should leave."

Lance smiled, but sweat on his brow glinted in a flash of lightning.

"Folks, folks. Settle down."

But the biddies crowded around the boy, touching him, questioning him.

A chair flipped over. A vase tumbled off the mantel, smashing on the floor. The shrieks and panicked footsteps nearly trampled the boy, Lance could hold none back as they fled through the house and out into the rain, some leaving coats behind.

The grandfather clock ticks in the new silence. Just me and Lance left.

Lance stands there. Then he sinks wearily into a chair. A lamp flicks on.

"You didn't have to go that far," he says, lighting a cigarette. "They'll expect that every year."

I yank the cigarette out of his mouth, and toss it toward the broken vase.

"Jesus," he says, standing. "Can't I get a break? It's hard work."

But I kick at the shards of the vase, and shake the wicker basket full of crumpled bills. He still can't hear me, but he knows me well enough to know what I mean.

"All right. Fine," he says, standing. "I'll get the dustpan. But I'm taking half of the cut this year. Don't mess with me, Mom. Your will says I can tear this all down and subdivide anytime I want."

He leaves the room. I watch him go. I sit, and Jacob drifts into the chair next to me. We laugh. No one hears us in the silence.

#

Seth Augenstein's fiction has appeared in *Writer's Digest*, *The Cracked Eye*, *Ginosko*, *Squalorly*, *The Kudzu Review*, as well as *The Molotov Cocktail* and other places. He spent a decade working at New Jersey newspapers and now writes about criminal forensics for magazines. His wife keeps him in a house upon a rocky ridge with a daughter, a dog, two cats, and innumerable dust bunnies.

Finding Moonlight

by James R. Gapinski

When the doctors finally released Mum, she was different. Little horns protruded from her forehead; she reeked of sulfur; her fingers twisted into spindly talons; she spoke gibberish and coughed up little plumes of smoke; if we left her wheelchair too close to a mousetrap or roach hotel, she'd eat the ensnared pests. *They must've mixed up the charts. That's not Mum*, Abby said. But I wasn't so sure. Mum's eyes were the same, with the same reddish glow that I remembered during bedtime stories.

There was this one story about a bear and a mouse who were friends, and something about the moon losing its moonlight, and the bear and mouse had to search the forest for a replacement light. I don't remember exactly how it all worked out, but I know for sure that it ended with the moon getting its light back—most kid's books have happy endings like that.

I pushed Mum's wheelchair into the bedroom while Abby telephoned doctors and nurses. I wiped some drool from Mum's mouth; I dabbed pus away from her horns. *We'll get you healthy*, I said. Mum replied with some more gibberish. I jotted down a few of Mum's better-enunciated words, though most were too quick and guttural for transcription. I tucked Mum into bed, set water on the nightstand, and took her temperature—still rising despite hourly ice baths. Once Mum was asleep, I searched for some of her gibberish on the internet. I got a few hits in Arabic, Latin, and Hebrew. The words *rain* and *blood* and *murder* and *terror* pinged back. There was also one hit for *love*, so I took that as a good sign.

By morning, Abby had shifted her efforts from doctors to priests, and by midday she convinced one to make a house call. The priest said *I've seen this before. I'll have your mother up and about in no time.* Mum screamed and spat bile onto his vestments. The priest held out his Bible. Mum began speaking English for the first time since her release. *Sinner, charlatan, deceiver*, she shouted, pointing at the priest. Then she began listing names and locations and dates. The priest ran from the house and kept going. Abby sat in her car and cried for a while.

I wheeled Mum into the living room and turned on one of those midday judge shows, like *Judge Judy* but with less yelling. I brushed her hair, and I asked *Mum, do you remember the story about the bear and the mouse? Do you know how they got a new light for the moon?* Mum nodded and said something unintelligible— it sounded more like pained moaning than a language.

Abby began looking up rabbis and Buddhist monks while a light bulb popped in the kitchen. Mum smiled. Some mouse entrails were caught in her front teeth. I got a toothpick and worked some of the guts away from her gum line. It was like a role reversal of childhood mac-n-cheese nights, back when Mum used to inspect my teeth after every third bite. I kissed Mum's warm forehead and placed my hand in hers. I stroked her bony fingers and said *The moon will be bright again soon. I promise.*

#

James R. Gapinski works as an adjunct Jedi, collects 8-bit video games, and edits *The Conium Review*. He also has some cats, which seems like a standard ingredient in most writer bio statements.

Prize Winners Vol. 2

Felons

The London Umbrella Company

by Jan Kaneen

The vibrations sink through the Plexiglas and marble, through the pavement, underneath the city that always sleeps, into my basement office. They're so loud down here, a million footsteps marching home. The heartbeats are louder though, cars and trains and tube carriages rammed with them aching, pulsing, throbbing.

You have to zone them out or you'd go mad, block them out by taking in every detail of the space around you, grey floor tiles below your feet, low plaster ceiling above your head, boarded on one side a hundred years ago against the lethal trickles of light that used to slink through the ventilation shaft. You had acolytes then, to do your bidding. Now, you watch the dark slivers of artificial light from the single bulb, study your ornate, mahogany desk and green velvet chair, the ebony filing cabinet, carved, Gothic, tall as a coffin, seven drawers high, all relics of opulence long gone. The distraction is fleeting so you switch focus to the black metal spike stabbing up from the desktop, set in a block of weighted oak, stuck with newspaper clippings almost to the top. You recall a very different use it was once put to, but not for long, the aching throb always draws you back. You try focusing on the job in hand, searching the quality newspapers, the *Times* and *Telegraph*, scouring the obituary columns, encircling names in black ink, cutting carefully around those earmarked for transcription.

"In memoriam," they say, the epitaphs to the great and good, "to Sir George Such-and-Such or The Right Honorable Lady Sarah...dearly departed...to be mourned at Cripplegate Church...or Bevis Marks Synagogue...on such a day...at such a time...send flowers to...charity donations accepted by...all inquiries addressed to..."

There are so many prestigious dead, a never-ending supply.

You address and seal the final envelope and place it on the pile of fifty others. You spike the fulfilled clipping and allow yourself to listen to the hubbub above. The after-dark sounds are back—the blather of night birds, scratch of rats, the stir of ghosts in long-forgotten graves deep beneath your feet—and you let the familiar gnaw start up. The city has decanted. It's time.

You walk round the piles of newspapers, turrets and battlements of them. They remind you of another home but your castle days are long past, you're smaller now, stooped and insignificant in your beige slacks, safely stripped back, your needs modest, no cooking, no abluting, no phone, no computer.

You go undetected in this all-seeing age.

You take your grey raincoat from the door hook and put it on, Count Nobody.

You pick up the post, unlock the door, take up your tatty Brigg umbrella made of hand-carved hickory wood and silk, your final concession to bygone grandeur, and go out into the night-lit corridor, the furthest corridor, deepest down, deserted by all but the shadows. No one chances this way even on the busiest workdays, beyond the hypnotic charms you wove to conceal your bones. The CCTV camera whirs as useless as mirrors.

You take the lift up and nod to the night watchman behind the reception desk, breathing deeply to stay in control. His pulse is deafening.

Outside, the italic rain falls slant. The city stinks. You open your umbrella and creep unseen through the deserted streets following the beat as the gnaw bites deeper. You post the envelopes into the pillar-box at Finsbury Circus. Fat raindrops fall from the city trees staining the envelopes darker white as you push them through the slit. You walk to the cashpoint, pay in today's cheques and withdraw £100. You're losing yourself to nature as you track the heartbeat to the burial ground at Bunhill Fields. You don't check for witnesses. If anyone was watching you'd feel it acutely, like pain.

You leap the railings, striding in time to the pulse under the monument, among the rubbish, wrapped in cardboard, stinking of gin and tobacco and urine. It smells delicious. You close your umbrella, slowly.

You kill at first penetration, an immediate climax, using fore and hind fangs, slicing through arteries and vertebrae alike. No telltale signs or markings of other Nosferati. Sated, you stand tall once more, then soar, flashing through cloud above the rain into a clearer night where the moon and stars shine bright white light. You fly fast and free, the icy wind in your face.

At the all-night 7-Eleven, you pick up newspapers, stamps, envelopes.

Back indoors, you nod to a different doorman. The guard has changed.

"Regular as clockwork, Sir," he says tapping his watch, his pulse bearable. He hands you yesterday's post.

Back in the office, you sit at your desk, open the *Times* and noose the names of the deceased elite. You make out each invoice for £10, add a condolence slip, "Sorry for your loss…hate to bother you at this sad time…umbrella repair outstanding…make cheques payable to…The London Umbrella Company."

They always pay, the privileged bereaved. Who would query something so commonplace among the well-to-do? It's a small, victimless crime devised to always go undetected. Ironic really, the dead maintaining the undead.

You sense the imminent sunrise, the returning herd, feel the coming of their blood and turn to the filing cabinet. The drawers are a counterfeit door. You step into the waiting shade and rest, in something like peace.

#

Jan Kaneen is doing an MA in Creative Writing at the Open University in the UK. She writes teeny weird stuff as an antidote to academia and to get match fit as she writes her first novel. Her surname is *Kaneen* despite many typos to the contrary.

Postmaster

by Henry Whittier-Ferguson

"The problem is that the goddamn Chinese keep stealing our secrets," says the man in the suit into his phone. "No. No, that's what I'm saying. I don't trust email. I'm at the post office. I'm mailing it now." He hands me the package he's holding. "Nevada," he says to me. "Can you overnight this?"

"It's going to cost you," I tell him. I am not Chinese but this is what I think: a secret is only a secret if it wants to be stolen. The man pays with a golden card. The package feels like a thick ream of paper. Back in the mailroom, I open it as a surgeon might open up a body.

Inside I find a stack of patents for a new kind of battery. These batteries charge faster and last longer. They can go in your phone or your computer or your car or your house. They can go in anything. The applications are limitless, the patents say. I photocopy each page and bind my copies together. When I'm done, I carefully reseal the package. Even I can't tell if it's been opened.

*

This kid was mailing drugs. His eyes were all over the room, pupils like dimes, and he was swallowing too much. I took his package home for the night. It turned out he was sending a copy of *Walden* with sheets of blotter acid between the pages. I ate a hit of the acid and sat in my armchair, reading the section called "Reading."

...and all the centuries to come shall have successively deposited their trophies in the forum of the world, I read. *By such a pile we may hope to scale heaven at last.*

I could feel my jaw hanging loose from my skull, my tongue soft and heavy, like wet newsprint. I went to the basement, where I keep all the secrets I know. I poured over them, my trophies.

I found the invoices from Rodney at the medical supply company, the itemized lists of gauze and antibiotics, sterilized needles and tubing and the sutures and titanium screws to keep the skin and bone together. I read Shane Bradley's W2 from his line cook job at the hotel. I knew his Social Security Number and how much he made last year, which was $27,432.86 before taxes. I read Melissa's postcard to Jesse while he was away at summer camp. She was sorry but she couldn't wait another month for him to come home, she was with Daniel now.

Some of them, I could see their faces as clear as when they handed me the letters. Others I never saw. I just picked their words out of a bin. I loved them all. My vision swam with hexagons of light, their edges diffusing into little rainbows. I felt like a prism, separating beams into spectrums, each color standing alone, even as it bled into the next.

*

The library burned blue-green because of all the ink. They said it might have been arson, though they could never be sure.

My mother was a librarian. I was twelve years old. I had grown up sneaking between the stacks, hiding in the dim room where they kept the microfilm and the projectors. The night it happened, they called her and we drove down and watched it all burn from behind the police barrier and I was sure that all was lost. I remember the exact sound of her cry as the roof finally caved, the groan of beams bending and the great sigh of heat that drew the moisture from my open mouth.

*

The secret to the batteries is in how they fit the cells together, so you can keep on building them as big as you want them to be. It's a good system. Sometimes you don't know what you're building until you've already built it. How can you know beforehand how big it will get?

I walk home through the park in the early evening, the copied pages safe in my bag. The air smells like sap and the sun moves through the trees in diagonals of shadow and light on the gravel path. An old man is searching through a trash can for empty bottles.

"Excuse me, are you Chinese?" I ask. He shakes his head.

"Oh. That's okay," I tell him. "Do you want to hear a secret?"

#

Henry Whittier-Ferguson is a maker of things with words and sounds and clay. A transplanted Michigander, he studied writing at Lewis & Clark College and continues to live in Portland, Oregon. You can find more of his work at www.itsthewhat.com.

Blood Feather and Soft Feather

by Melissa Monks

This way. And that way. The thing wasn't shiny. Soft Feather wanted shiny. In the nest it should be shiny. He chided. And chided. Too near him, Blood Feather shifted from foot to foot to foot to foot. The not-shiny thing was a troubling mystery. Soft Feather chided. Blood Feather shifted. Soft Feather rubbed his head into the not-shiny thing's fat pinkness. Smooth. Still warm. Half furry. Soft Feather regarded Blood Feather. This way and that. Blood Feather was a troubling mystery herself. Every crow knows that a thing can be understood, even the not-shiny, half-furry things, if one looks at them this way and that way. But perhaps not Blood Feather. Blood Feather shifted. Soft Feather explored. The not-shiny, half-furry thing had eyes. Front eyes, like the dirty no-feathers. The sky-cloggers. The river chokers. But it was too small. Soft Feather poked his beak, this time, at the not-shiny, half-furry thing's fat pinkness. Blood Feather shifted. This way. And that. The pinkness gave. Then came back. Like an all-furry thing. But so small for a front-eye. And incomplete. It dripped. Soft Feather suspected its smallness and incompleteness were dependent upon each other. Soft Feather regarded Blood Feather. She spread her wings. He chided. She folded. She shifted. This way and that.

Blood Feather urged. Soft Feather stabbed a front eye. This way. Bluer. That way. It held the sky. His beak sunk in the soft, watery meat. And it was good. But troubling. Soft Feather pulled his beak from the eye. Sucking. Dripping. Blood Feather shifted. This way. And that. The size. The size, Blood Feather. How did you get one this size? This way. Blood Feather tugged golden, curly fur. She urged. Across the nest. That way. Red. Soft Feather conceded. Indeed, it filled the nest. Flowed and overflowed. Dripped. And dripped. So, not that small.

This way. Blood Feather urged. Soft Feather pushed his beak into the dripping dripping dripping end of the not-shiny, half-furry thing. And it was warm. Soft Feather withdrew. That way. Soft Feather regarded Blood Feather. He chided. Conceded. She shifted.

This way. Soft Feather paused. Soft Feather listened. Something shrill in the distance. That way.

"My baby! My baby!" Blood Feather mimicked. Soft Feather regarded Blood Feather. A food thing, then. Soft Feather ate. Blood Feather shifted.

#

Melissa Monks writes and lives in a world of her own. It's hardly ever a nice place, but it's hers. Her work also appears in *Quantum Fairy Tales* and *The Literary Hatchet*.

Everything Must Go

by Emily Livingstone

    Laura reached into the purse and unfolded the wallet with a practiced hand. She removed the cash.
    Her phone trumpeted an alert. A sale. Someone was getting a steal: her mother's antique bowl, a prized possession of Grammy Lola's. Sold for $25. No reserve. Laura had other items listed, too: the blue cable-knit sweater that her mother wore for casual gatherings, the watercolor that hung in the bathroom, a silver ashtray, and a photo album of Laura's baby pictures. Ten people were watching the album. People were freaks.
    "Why is the television on?" her mother called from the den. "Who left it on?"
    Laura shut it off.
    Her mother said, "Where's Charlie?"
    "Charlie's going to be on television," Laura said. "He saved a child from drowning."
    "On television? My Charlie. Turn it on."
    Her mother focused on the screen as it flashed with people running, people eating disgusting pizza, and people looking grim because "the Shingles virus is already inside" them.

Sometimes, Laura said Charlie was at work. Sometimes, he was at the library. Once, he was cheating on his wife with a bimbo in a cheap motel. Once, Laura told the truth: that her precious brother was dead. Her mother had cried for an hour and broken things. She'd suddenly remembered Laura's name and cursed her.

Well, she could curse all she wanted. Her life was disappearing around her: past, present, and future.

"Will you get my purse?"

"Sure, Mom."

Her mother checked her wallet. "I need to go out. I need to get things."

"Sure, we will."

"Where's Charlie?"

"At the playground, on the monkey bars."

"What would he be doing there?"

Laura walked away. She started packaging the bowl, surrounding it in bubble wrap and newspaper. She made out the address label and closed up the box.

There was a little rush of satisfaction.

Then there was a pang of anxiety. All her eBay auctions but one would end in an hour. The last auction would end in three.

It was time to get ready. She took the two diaries, hers and her mother's, and laid them in bubble wrap, ready to ship. She took a Polaroid of herself with Charlie's old camera, and put that on top. Flipping open her laptop, she checked the posting. "What My Mother Has Forgotten and I Haven't." Description: two diaries, one Polaroid.

She left the computer open to the page and went to the kitchen. She plugged in the blender. She dumped in the raspberries and strawberries from the crisper drawer. She added all the pills from her mother's bottle with its myriad warning labels. Hand over the lid, she pressed "Pulse," and it became a sickening, bloody-looking mess. She added ice. More grinding. Laura stuck it in the fridge. Not yet. Not until the packages were ready.

She texted the boy down the street who did errands for her: *Packages to go out. Will leave them on porch with your cash in envelope. Must go out today. Thanks.*

There were already five watchers and one bid: $2.63. Why $2.63? Laura scratched at her wrist, an old habit. $2.63 for the story of the day she came to her mother, when she was only fifteen, with a problem—nausea, a test, the deep need of a daughter for her mother. The day her mother brought her to get it taken care of. The day her mother stopped looking at her straight-on. They'd both written about it. It was something Laura had picked up from her mother—the driving need to document in secret all that occurred. She'd thought—surely her mother hadn't really stop loving her—she'd hoped—but then she'd read the entry from that day. *Laura to doctor's.* That was all it said. The next day: *Laura unbearably weepy today. Sent her to her room.* Then, nothing. No mention of Laura in the diaries again. Ever.

Laura looked at the screen. A new bid: $14.99. Two hours and twelve minutes to go. There was a reserve of $25.01, and she wasn't going to let it go for less than that. If someone wanted to read this—to try to piece it together like a detective on a *48 Hours* episode—there should be a price, and it should be more than a stupid bowl. God knows, there was a price for Laura, and there would be for her mother. Two hours and ten minutes to go.

#

Emily Livingstone is a high school teacher and writer living with her husband, daughter, and German Shepherd. In the quiet moments, and sometimes even the not-so-quiet, she writes. You can also find her at emilylivingstone.wordpress.com.

Beyond the Briars

by Joshua Patterson

If I hadn't seen it for myself—hell, if Tommy Howard hadn't been there to see it too—then I would never have believed it existed. I'm still not sure that I do. Enough time has passed where the days of running around the abandoned train tracks seemed more like an old movie than something I had lived. Too many freezes and thaws had left no more then a grainy glimpse of the rusted trestle over the Susquehanna. Cue marks loomed over the crabgrass growing between the rocks of the rail and a deep vignette surrounded the path that lead down to that...thing.

"You first, Robbie," I could hear Tom say in his soft and girlish prepubescent voice, and then the film reel burns up. The final memory too terrifying for a mind to hold on to except for in the deepest and darkest of dreams.

Tommy and I hadn't really talked after that day. We tried to hang out like we always did; begging for change outside of Bob's Diner and harassing the girls at the Galaxy Bowl until they gave us a free game. We even pilfered a few smokes off Tommy's parents to drag on behind the bleachers at the football field, but something felt different. Something had changed between us. Looking back on it now, I suppose that we believed the distance would make it feel like it hadn't happened at all. If I could forget Tommy Howard, then I could forget everything that lived past those briars on that lonely path beyond the trestle. That had been almost twenty years ago, but I still hadn't forgotten. That scene from the old movie of my life circled around and around like the lever of a twisted jack in the box—never knowing when the thing was going to jump back out.

"How much further?" the detective barks.

We hadn't even made it past the Thatcher property and onto the tracks, but the detective was on to something, the trip did feel longer than I remembered. The stolen cigarettes of youth had turned into a pack a day habit, and though I felt winded trotting through the long grass and uneven divots of the cow-field that led to the railroad, the anticipation of what may be waiting on the other side of this trek made it seem endless. For the detective there was the promise of a body, the final piece of evidence for the prosecution, and for me—I suppose there would be something similar. I shook my head and we continued walking towards the rails with the falling sun on our backs and the spring's first choir of crickets buzzing around us.

Before the detectives, the headlines and that ominous letter, the last I had heard of Tommy Howard, delivered straight from the gossip queen of the Tri-State area herself—my mother—was that Tommy was doing well. He had shacked up with Stacey Pearson and was teaching music at Sidney High. This, of course, was followed with *Why couldn't you have stayed here and done something like Tommy had*, and *Whatever happened to you two? You boys were as thick as thieves.* The back-home news: where the names were familiar and the guilt was always thicker than ever. After Stacey went missing, however, my mother changed her tune; she *always knew that boy was trouble, and she was glad I had been smart enough to stay away from him.* If only that last part were true, I thought to myself.

A flood of nostalgia struck me as the tracks came into view. Tommy and I playing guns, tossing rocks at the boxcars as they chugged past to see what kind of sounds they made and testing how long we could keep our balance running up and down the rails. How could I believe that the innocent little boy on the tracks could have grown up to kill his wife?

"Keep it moving."

Rob, the letter had read, *if they come asking, show them where it is. – T.H.*

As the detective and I reached the trestle, the old black-and-white film in my head was starting to color in. The last of the good memories—Tommy and I spitting over the sides of the old wooden frame and into the creek bed below—would stop at the end of that bridge. The jack-in-the-box was winding, and it cranked over with every beat of my pulse. More than anything, I didn't want to see what was inside.
"We're close," I tell him.

The temperature dropped as the wind blew casually between the beams, but it wasn't cold enough for the goosebumps that were rising up on my arms. The air was stale, and the taste of ozone lingered from some leftover storm. My feet turned to concrete, and I wanted to stop, but I had to know. *Was it still there? Had it ever been there to begin with, or was it all just the overactive imagination of two bored preteens?* Up ahead I could see a small path carved out among the overgrowth, and an image of yellow fangs and matted fur raged into my thoughts. It wasn't human.

"Well, where is she?" the detective asks. "I hope for your sake that you're not wasting my time."

...if they come asking, show them where it is.

I point my shaky finger towards the path, and watch the detective work his way through the weeds.

"It's just beyond the briars."

#

Joshua Patterson is a horror writer with a fondness for the dark and dreary. He is a New York native but is currently living in Portland, Oregon, because of that whole dark and dreary thing.

The Sitting Room

by Aeryn Rudel

The place he called the sitting room was cool and dry, with concrete walls and floor. The smell was pungent, but it never bothered him. It reminded him of the good work he'd done, how his collection had grown, and how each piece had changed over time.

A single chair was precisely positioned in the center of the room and allowed him to view the installation from a comfortable distance. He would sit for hours, pondering the changes that had taken place since his last visit. He allowed himself into the sitting room once a week; more than that and he feared it would lose its magic, its soothing nature. He longed for it constantly, though, and the need made it all the more satisfying when he finally went down and sat.

His sanctuary was an old fallout shelter that had come with the house he'd bought a few years ago. The entrance had been sealed over, and the realtor hadn't known it was there. He'd stumbled upon it while remodeling and had immediately recognized its potential. It was isolated and quiet, a place made for private display. Before, he'd done his work where he'd found it, leaving little time to revel in the experience. It had to be quick, sudden, ugly—and these early endeavors were now lost to him. The sitting room allowed him to linger over each new work, soaking it in for as long as he liked.

This was the second time he'd visited the sitting room this week, but today was an exception. He had something new to display, and he wanted to get it up on the wall and part of the installation as soon as possible. He'd dragged it down to the room in a burlap sack. It was big, and it would be difficult to mount, but he'd made the necessary preparations.

He stood in the center of the room, behind the chair, the new piece at his feet. He knew he'd made the right decision. The installation, while still beautiful, had begun to look incomplete. He always felt this way just before he added something new; a sense of the unfinished and a lack of purpose that only new work would drive away.

He untied the burlap sack and grabbed hold of the piece. It left a red smear on the concrete as he dragged it toward the display wall. That bothered him. Colors went on the wall not on the floor.

The tools he needed where at the base of the installation: a four-pound sledgehammer, four stainless steel spikes, each six inches long, and a U-shaped bolt, eight inches long and four inches wide, sharpened on both ends. They were ordinary objects—things you could pick up at any Home Depot— augmented for his purposes. He had a sturdy block and tackle bolted to the ceiling that allowed him to raise a new work by its arms so it could be secured to the wall. He positioned his latest piece roughly three feet from the floor, then anchored the rope. He started with the U-bolt. It provided the most stability. He carefully positioned it beneath the solar plexus with one hand and raised the sledge with the other. He struck a sharp, firm blow, and the twin spikes sank into the piece a good half-inch. Its eyes flew open at the shock and pain. This irritated him—it made the mounting more difficult when they squirmed. He much preferred they awaken during the viewing period; then their movements only added to the work.

The new piece opened its mouth to speak or scream, but both lungs had been perforated and nothing came out but a trickle of blood and a rattling gasp. He continued to hammer at the bolt until it had penetrated the flesh and bone and the wall behind it. The new piece thrashed the entire time, splattering him with its fluids. Finally, he'd had enough, and he smashed the sledgehammer into the side of its head. He heard a dull crunch—the skull fracturing—and the new piece went limp. He frowned; too hard. He hoped that wouldn't affect its aesthetic positioning on the wall or how it painted.

He did the feet next, hammering a steel spike through each instep. With the feet secured, he moved on to the wrists, one spike just below each hand. The new piece was secured to the wall, and already it had begun to paint, staining the concrete red behind it. In time, he'd make more holes to let other colors out—greens, browns, more reds.

He glanced along the wall where his previous works hung. The one next to the newest had begun to turn gray, and its painting had become muted. Farther along, the paintings grew more and more subdued, and the pieces themselves became withered and shrunken, completing their purpose. The new piece stood out from them, bold and exquisite, a shining monarch of color among its tired gray subjects.

There was still much to do, but the chair beckoned him. He would sit for a while and watch the colors flow.

#

Aeryn Rudel is a freelance writer from Seattle, Washington. He is a notorious dinosaur nerd, a rare polearms expert, a baseball connoisseur, and he has mastered the art of fighting with sword-shaped objects (but not actual swords). Aeryn's first novel, *Flashpoint*, was recently published by Privateer Press, and he occasionally offers dubious advice on the subjects of writing and rejection (mostly rejection) on his blog at www.rejectomancy.com.

Jokers to the Right

by Rich Larson

"Prove you're a real clown or we feed you your balls." That's how the interrogation starts, once the grocery bag duct-taped around his head is torn off and Javier finds himself in some filthy mold-bloomed backroom. If his legs weren't lashed to a chair with electrical cord, his knees would be knocking together. He is sweating madly under his makeup.

There are two of them, and Javier managed to glean names from their arguing while he was slamming around in the backseat. Nacho is the one who wants to feed him testicles; he's a wiry type with squinty eyes and a shaved head. Paco is fatter and slightly calmer. Both of them are covered in tattoos Javier recognizes as Mara.

But Javier has had nothing to do with that life for decades. Javier is Bonzo the Clown, now, beloved private performer, and someone has made a gigantic fucking mistake that might soon cost him his genitals. If he'd known, he would have finished off the Don Julio bottle before he left his flat instead of finishing off the Hacienda.

"Why would I not be a real clown?" he says hoarsely.

"Why?" Nacho snaps. "Because a half-hour ago, a hitter dressed up like a clown wasted El Patron at his grandson's birthday party. His birthday party!" Tears well in the thug's eyes; Paco puts a hand on his shoulder. "That little kid, he watched his abuelo die right in front of him, and now he gonna be scarred for life, you know?"

"I know, vato, I know," Paco says gently. Then he turns back to Javier and bares his teeth. "The hitter bails out the backyard, and now we find you a block away. Just a big coincidence, right? Bet you dumped the piece in that manhole on Juarez."

"I was on my way to a client's party," Javier says. "Calle Bombona. I swear to God."

"Yeah, yeah, you said that, but we drove past Bombona and we ain't seen no party on Bombona." Paco points to Nacho, who is still sniffling as he flicks his butterfly knife open. "Why's that, huh?"

"It was a private thing." Javier swallows. "You know. Private party."

"No, I don't know," Paco says. "Private parties still have balloons and loudspeakers and shit." Suddenly, his eyes narrow. "Wait, you mean clown sex?"

"No!" Javier snaps. "Look, I got the call, they paid the deposit, and I was supposed to show up at three o'clock, okay?"

"If you're a clown, tell us a joke," Nacho says thickly, holding up the knife. "A good joke."

"I, ah, I do more physical humor."

"Like when someone hits you with a hammer? Or slices off your slimy, lying tongue?"

Javier blanches. "How does a Guatemalan get into an honest business?" he blurts. "Through the window! Ha! Through the window, see?"

Nacho frowns. "I got cousins from Guatemala."

"Yeah, that shit is racist," Paco chimes in. "Clowns aren't racist. They're innocent. They make kid jokes."

Nacho lowers his voice. "Paco, man, should we try calling Raul again? This has to be the guy, right? You already seen that tat on his neck, bullshit he a clown."

"I ain't calling until we're sure," Paco whispers back. "Have to make him cop to it."

Javier is trembling all over as Nacho approaches.

"All right. Physical humor. If you're a clown, you should be able to juggle."

"I can!" Javier says, voice stretched to a squeak. "Five clubs, nine balls, just get the stuff out of my bag and I'll—"

"Balls," Nacho says, waggling the butterfly knife. "We're going to slice off your balls, and then you're going to juggle them for us, okay?" He reaches down and yanks Javier's bright yellow pants down his hairy pale thighs.

"Wait!" Javier screams. "Wait, wait! I'll tell you what I know!" He slumps on the chair, heart hammering his ribs.

"Yeah?" Nacho demands.

"You need three balls minimum to juggle," Javier says slowly. "So one of you will have to contribute a testicle."

Nacho's reply is interrupted by the door swinging open behind them, framing a dark-haired man with a janitor's mop and shocked expression. Javier pleads with his eyes.

"Perdón," the janitor mumbles, skewering Javier's last hope. "I'll...go."

"Fucking right you will," Paco says.

Then his head blows apart, splattering Javier's lap with greasy blood and gray matter. Javier, stunned, watches him rag doll to the floor. He's so deafened by the first shot that he doesn't realize there was a second until Nacho falls, too.

Javier looks up, and the dark-haired man is striding forward, cupping a black handgun. He pauses to put another bullet into Nacho's head, then sets to untying Javier.

"Gracias a Dios," Javier mumbles, realizing he's been saved. "Oh, my God, they were going to kill me. Thank you, thank you." He can't actually hear himself speak through the ringing in his ears, but the man gives him a perfunctory nod. As he yanks up his pants, Javier notices a telltale smear of dark makeup around the man's eyes, some red still ringed around his mouth.

The man says something to him, and it takes a few goes before the indistinct burble turns into "Do you have wipes? Wipes in the bag?"

"Yeah," Javier says shakily, standing up. "It's a bitch to get off, isn't it?" His head is a carousel, and he asks, almost giddily, "Are you a clown, too? What are the chances?"

The man goes to the bag and uses a tuft of wet wipes from Javier's Ziplock stash.

"Thanks," he says.

He picks up Nacho's dropped pistol and shoots Javier in the head with it before setting it back down. Then he swaps his own weapon into Javier's twitching fingers, bundles up the electrical cords and briefs, and hurries out into the San Cabo sunshine.

#

Rich Larson was born in West Africa, has studied in Rhode Island and worked in Spain, and now writes from Grande Prairie, Alberta. His short work has been nominated for the Theodore Sturgeon, featured on io9, and appears in numerous Year's Best anthologies as well as in magazines such as *Asimov's*, *Analog*, *Clarkesworld*, *F&SF*, *Interzone*, *Strange Horizons*, *Lightspeed* and *Apex*. He was the most prolific author of short science fiction in 2015. Find him at richwlarson.tumblr.com.

Libertas

by Warren Buchanan

They told me she didn't have a heart, that she was just a statue. *She's French*, I said. *Of course she has a heart.* It had been pretty hard to get into her head for awhile now, but no one thought to guard her heart, so it was easy to get in there and take it. Now, it's in a shed in my backyard, in what was supposed to be a home gym, back when we had a home that we determined needed a gym. What's that old saying about where the heart is? Probably not pushed up against a weight bench covered in cobwebs and unopened, freshly-packed boxes stained with water damage from a leak in the roof. But that's where it is, all seven hundred pounds of it, thump-thumping away, driving me crazy.

God, that thumping. I wonder if anyone else can hear it. But even when that lawyer came over with paperwork for me to sign and he admired the house and the backyard and the view and he stood right there on the patio with those wicker chairs I'd never liked but Mary insisted we get for when we might be entertaining, he didn't seem to hear it. *Nice home you have here*, he said, and I wondered if he might correct himself after the fact. He didn't, though, and then he left, and he took his papers and said other people would be back another day to take the other things that the papers said needed to be taken (those boxes, for one) and he didn't once notice the giant metal heart I was keeping in my shed. Which is good, because he probably would have taken that, too.

On top of the thumping, the heart glows at night. It's a weird, dull, greenish glow. At least it is now. When I first brought it back, it had a copper tint to it like dirty blonde hair in the sunlight. Now, it's this greenish gleam that pokes at the seams of the shed where the rain gets in, and I can't sleep. I lie awake with my thoughts and I start to wonder why I even stole the damn thing in the first place. I think I had wanted to do it so that it would bring people back together again. Get people on both sides talking with one another, fighting for a common cause. *Where's the heart? Who would steal the heart? How do we get the heart back?* and so on. But it didn't work. Nobody was united. Things didn't get better. All that effort for nothing.

I think the heart's starting to wither. It looks smaller than before, like it's shriveling up, disappearing. The thump-thumping's gotten softer, and the glow at night is dimming. So much so that I can see the stars again. Mary and I used to admire them from the roof of her RV (the one we were going to take across the country to see the statue in the first place) while it sat parked in our driveway. We'd search for our favorite constellations. Hers was Ursa Major, mine was Orion. We always joked that those stars wouldn't get along if they were together. Afterwards, we'd make love on the floor of the mobile home, steps away from our large bed in our house, and just lay there. I'd stroke her hair and she'd kiss my neck and we'd make animal noises and talk in funny voices until the dawn's early light washed the stars away.

I'm planning on taking the heart back tomorrow. I'm going to use the RV, before I can't anymore. I know the only thing I can do now is give the heart back. It was never mine to begin with, anyway, and the ole gal needs it more than I do. I'm going to take the old route back to the coast, the one that cuts through the middle of everything. Maybe things have always been split in two, right from the beginning, and nobody ever really knew how to fix it. I can see myself stopping along the way, somewhere in the heart of the country, far away from the city lights. I climb up the fiberglass ladder to sit on top of the RV. I lie there and listen to the soft, sad heartbeat below me as I stare at the banner of stars above me, hunting for the bear.

#

Warren Buchanan is a Bay Area writer who writes short fiction, flash, novels and screenplays. He got his MFA from Saint Mary's College and a BA in Screenwriting from Loyola Marymount. His mother is very proud of him.

The Noose on the Roof

by Charles Scott

The noose on the roof is always there.
It's tied to a hook that's attached to the garage. The noose doesn't hang. The open end is thrown on top of the roof. Somehow, it's more intimidating that way.
We could see the rope from our room on the second floor. The window faced the backyard where the garage is. When we were bad, Dad pointed out the window. He told us it had been used before.
Other parents might put a stool in the corner and threaten their kids with a timeout. Other kids might go to bed without dinner. Our dad pointed out the window. We looked.
Every January and every July, Dad took us out to the garage. We'd stand with our backs to a support beam and he'd put a notch in the wood with his knife and tell us how much we had grown. I grew three inches one time. Dad pulled the rope off the roof, cut three inches, and threw it back. He did that every time. We'd get taller and the rope would get shorter.
When we got older, he'd send us out by ourselves. We'd mark a notch and we'd cut the rope. We'd throw it back on the roof. He'd watch.

The neighbors would complain. They'd come over and Dad would give them a beer and they'd talk. Then they'd leave. Dad said a few beers could solve any problem. I thought a few beers caused most of them.

We had a lot of new neighbors. I don't think anyone wanted to live by us.

I didn't know my mom. I knew how tall she was though. There was a notch on the beam. When I was a kid I didn't think that was weird. We all had one. It's what we did.

When I told Dad I'd reached her notch, he smiled. He said he had a rope that long already. I took the rope down from the roof and made a cut anyway. He said he didn't want to use the one that was cut already. He said it was his.

When I was fifteen, I reached my dad's height. When I told Dad, he did not smile. I still have that rope. It's mine.

I own the house now. The kids in the room are mine. I don't drink. The neighbors like me. We still go out to the garage twice a year and put a notch in the wood.

My kids are well-behaved, much better than we were. They're well-adjusted too. When they're bad, we send them to a stool in their room for a timeout. They sit on the stool and look out the same window we did.

The noose on the roof is always there.

#

Husband, brother, son, uncle, cat hoarder, and Cubs season ticket holder, Charles Scott also plays competitive skee ball in Chicago.

Space Monkey Mafia

by Allison Spector

They say enough monkeys with enough typewriters will recreate the works of Shakespeare. But that's not why I'm here. I ain't that kind of primate. The pay in the writer racket is terrible—and fuck it anyhow, I'll leave the humanities to the humans.

The reason why I'm cooped up in this filthy safe house with nothing to drink but bottom shelf vodka is cause I'm a cheeky little monkey, and more curious than George. That curiosity and an uncommonly high IQ earned me a gig as a cosmonaut back in the early '90s. I was the last furry bastard to take a trip into the black. I was also the only one to improve upon the orbital maneuvering system and take a joyride while I was up there. After the USSR's collapse, I was passed around like a cheap cigar from one defunct official to the next, though they mostly saw me as a mascot—a fuzzy souvenir. They never understood what a glorious little motherfucker I really was. What scares the shit out of me is that these guys do.

"Vesta! What the fuck you doing?" the fat man with the sweaty, red face asks as he ripples towards me. "We got you a goddamned Hermes 3000 typewriter—a classic—to give us something worth what we paid for you. And all you type is 'more vodka.' You think this is Club Med or something?" I raise my bottle of Kulov in my left paw and a furry middle finger to go along with it. Boris Badass replies with a punch that lands so hard I'm launched into space all over again—but only for a moment.

"We ain't playing, you little shit-thrower," my pal continues, in Russian this time. "You've been around some of the premier scientists, spooks, engineers and ex-pats in the Old Country. We know it was you that took the *Aleksandra* for a joyride. We know you have an IQ higher than most of the eggheads you worked with. You gotta have something we can use to get ahead. I'm not expecting a nuclear bomb, but a good rocket fuel recipe might keep us from sending you to a cosmetics lab."

Rocket fuel recipe. These guys are pure bloody amateurs. I raise my hand to my face and a sliver of blood rubs off on the back of my paw. My head hurts like a motherfucker, and for once it isn't from the Kulov. I stare at the Hermes 3000 and take a swig of my Russian mother's milk. I should hate this bastard, but for some reason I can't. Maybe it's the Stockholm Syndrome, or the booze, or the desire to show off, but I feel the hubris rising in my chest—the desire to impress—the desire to be loved.

"Nuclear is child's play, Comrade" I type on the shiny vintage keyboard, "I also got Granny Stalin's finest meth recipe and a dozen launch codes." I offer a quick spec sheet on a dirty bomb, my furry little fingers flying at breakneck pace.

Then I type the punchline. Five magic words. "But what's in it for me?"

Boris's face takes on a strange expression. "What's in it for you? You ask me what's in it for *you*?" He reaches a meaty hand around my neck, and for a moment I think I'm done for. Instead, he slaps me approvingly on the shoulder and pats my cheek. "You got real balls, Vesta. I like that. We're just humble businessmen, little fella, but one day we'll be kings. When that happens, you'll be King of the Motherfucking Monkeys."

"Queen," I type in reply.

"What?"

"I'm a girl monkey."

"Oh," Boris says blankly. "Shouldn't have punched a girl. Sorry about that."

I shrug. "Being queen might help me forget," I type, "but I'll expect to be paid cash money for my contribution. And I want my own mooks."

"Eh, why the fuck not," Boris decides, extending his hand to shake. "You give us half that shit you just mentioned and you got yourself a deal."

They say enough monkeys with typewriters will recreate the works of Shakespeare. Me? I'm about to rule the motherfucking world.

#

Allison Spector is a New Jersey expat who was banished due to a spray tan allergy. Her work has been published with *1888, Longridge Review, Moonglasses Magazine*, and other fine purveyors of whimsy. You can check out her weird words at allisonspector.com.

Prize Winners Vol. 2

Shadows

The Devil's Taken His Dress Off
After Santiago Caruso

by Amanda Chiado

It's all in what you worship, the delicate shift in darkness
when you enter a sacred room that is strung up with a body
that indefinitely has its mouth gaping, to let spirits in or out—
to offer a portal for prayers that vibrate within the bones
of the house. All the disbelievers are braided like history,
trailing away tears in the hurricane. Without hushing, wear the loveliest
of recollections, the ghosts of animals who breathe necessity,
who whisper their songs like a hot exhalation in the desert
dawn.
If you hear water, the devil's taken his dress off. If you hear laughter,
you are not close enough. Something is in danger, and when it is you,
we will send you up on the weight of a flame, repeat
tremendous the error
of your being, and then drop you like a meteor, meaningless. If no one
cares for you, the devil loses interest. Worship is a wage, a barter.
If you want to be swept up in the crime, wave your barrel

like you're never going to be seen again—a mother wants to stop
the incidentals, and blood. My gathered hands are a compass seeking the light which renders itself in forms of confession. My knees are pools of weight—towers of exit, chamber, cylinder,
click, release. We can agree I have been so wrong, kissing the fists
that in the dark were shaped like wings–but light, light is ever king.

#

Upon a delicate throne constructed from the cheesiest Cheetos, Amanda cheers her strange, miniature royalty. Isabella and Gianluca wade and coo in an hourglass-shaped pool filled with gobs of earwax-colored, edible slime. Fabio, the king of the castle chuckles from atop the world's largest meatball holding his pitchfork and all, all is right with the world. Get weirder at www.amandachiado.com.

stark raving naked

by Christopher P. Mooney

This city in the early hours reminds me of the dawn streets of
my yearning childhood
with its brown-stone tenements caked with mud and grime
and putrid semen
trodden on by barefoot angels starved for attention with guts
swollen on lard
The empty silver lifts with illiterate obscenities scrawled on
filthy damp hollow walls
reek of wanton poverty take-away vomit and alcohol piss

Thick darkness and naked madness are everywhere and all
around
as we sift through the wasteland detritus in broken-down
alleys of eternal sadness
where intoxicated juveniles gnash rotted teeth at the uniforms
cool-cat hipsters turn tricks for gas money under yellow street
lamps
and the pungent smell of cheap dope lingers always
in the dull bluish haze of lost souls and dead abandoned lives

The houses are eternal tombs and the beds mere graves
that play unwilling host to vast human souls laid bare to life's carnage
who gave it all over for the quick hit the short con the long night
amid the sounds of ghoulish screams that could fill Golgothan valleys
and non-stop violent talk where nothing is said
as voids are pondered over and filled and emptied again

Suicide dames with bleached hair bawl in empty movie theatres
and bored subway drivers long for the body in flight
Soup and sodomy are on the menu tonight
Naked flesh will be chewed slurped eaten
and we will choke on the wet porcelain bones of other people's straight-jacketed dreams

Time marches forward with booted feet on gravel
cast-iron ashtrays overflow with the doubts of the nearby world
and torn remnants of first-draft poems float away in the damp air
as I suck turpentine dregs from plastic bottles
aching for the end of nightmarish day and maybe for the end of it all

#

Christopher P. Mooney was born and raised in Glasgow, Scotland, and currently lives and writes in a small house near London, England. Information on his published stories and poems can be found at playingwiththepoem.wordpress.com and via Twitter (@ChrisPatMooney).

Children of the Damp

by B.T. Schweitzer

Covered in the rags of waxy coated scraps of foil left in a garbage heap they toil in the forest by the interstate crossing. Unseen save by the light of fireflies, and flashes of headlights through the trees in the ichor of the night they dance. In the rhythm of the rain to the tune of the spheres overhead and those between his legs they are a shapeless ballet of mushrooms and moonbeams. Neither animal, nor plant, nor man, they are too fine for that and made of the same rib cage as Eve. Gently cracking the bones of every tree and peeling open the petals of each flower through the sickly sweet adoration of halitosis kisses. Even painting the dew droplets on the leaves of grass with brushes made from the hair of blind moths more white than milk and louder than David Bowie playing electrical guitar on Mars. While their cousins dab sand in the eyes of little boys and little girls this goblin ilk takes the shape of one hundred beetles innumerable and exact to consume the fallen stag and return it to their home—the Damp. Decadence in dirt, this palace of bones and rot lies beneath the surface of every puddle in a microcosm that sterile men in white coats have observed but never seen. Behind the turn of every leaf as the final chords of summer's ballad die in the air their numbers rise upon the lunar horizon. Like any colony of hymenoptera scurrying efficiently in the subterranean wasteland of boogeymen and toddlers these children feast hungrily upon the remains of their parents emptying fleshy husks to cover their white skin and red eyes until they return to the land of the living at a quarter past eight for the morning commute.

#

Brett-Thomas Schweitzer is a 24-year-old horror, science fiction, and fantasy author living in Denver, Colorado. Specializing in very tiny works he writes two-sentence and six-word stories as well as flash fiction. Over 700 such works can be found on his website www.BTSchweitzer.com and his flash fiction has been published by *The Molotov Cocktail*.

The Divine Heap
After Sam Gibbons

by Amanda Chiado

I am a thousand body bags heavy with heart. My mother says, "You are all of these trinkets." I stand upon the hoarders' tower like a death drag. I want to unzip my collection into a deeper backlash of plastic devils. The original black was an opaque white. There is a crest to this oblivion and the mushroom skirts hover like the know-better. There isn't any supervision in this intermediary, but cardboard dreamscapes, crushable keeping. You cannot save me here where the Sasquatch hunts me instead. I was born to be a doll and maybe that is the echo of hunger here, among these iceberg guts. I was trying to become that hiker who is propelled by her weight, who shoves away from the lava, who is a winged triumphant instead of a whore without a head. The screaming was supposed to be a fan that shot me into beauty. Even when I tiptoe on my divine heap, gently enough, as if were my mother's body, it continues to shift and roar, and the marionette strings that once tethered me to life, now are losing their starting point. I dig into my burden for an engine. I swim toward the surface; even the bricks stuck to my feet want to taste heaven.

#

Upon a delicate throne constructed from the cheesiest Cheetos, Amanda cheers her strange, miniature royalty. Isabella and Gianluca wade and coo in an hourglass shaped pool filled with gobs of earwax-colored, edible slime. Fabio, the king of the castle chuckles from atop the world's largest meatball holding his pitchfork and all, all is right with the world. Get weirder at www.amandachiado.com.

Mud Ceremony

by Sara Ryan

Today, the jackal marries
the fox. The fox is dead,
but still red as a split lip—
a clumsy pair.

The jackal is a witch kissing
her wife—the sunshower
wets her fur like a compulsion
of storm, of sun beat to blue
fire. A bright devil.

There are many things I have never done.
Buy a lottery ticket. Call
a radio station. Play slots.
Catch a bouquet of wisteria
or rats. A plague. Maybe

I'm the witch—the wolf
in a wedding dress. I can't
say why the crow I marry

isn't in the folklore—
isn't in the black book.

When the rain spills from
the sky's mouth like milk—
somewhere, a wife is crying.
Maybe I'm the wife. The devil
beating me, fighting
over my chicken bone;

bloody, stripped of meat.
This is when the funfair
begins. When the weather
turns salty—whips the dead
fox redder.

#

Sara Ryan is a second-year poetry MFA candidate at Northern Michigan University and an associate editor of poetry for *Passages North*. Her poetry has been published in *Boxcar Poetry Review, The Boiler Journal, Reservoir Journal, Hermeneutic Chaos* and others, and is also forthcoming from *Tinderbox, Storm Cellar,* and *The Grief Diaries*. She writes about spooky phenomena, Scandinavian myth, and witches.

Visitation

by Frances Klein

The angels are hungry.
They roost at the kitchen table—
haloed by streetlights—
eating ham sandwiches
made with leftover ham, hold the mustard.

Their wings are ragged. Mud and leaves
ornament the lice-matted feathers.
They try to keep them tucked
off the floor, muttering mea culpas
around mouthfuls of bread.

You make up the guest room,
the trundle-bed, the couch.
Each pulls on the old nightclothes
that belonged to your husband,
shirts backward, unbuttoned.

Late morning the angels awaken.
They flock around the coffee pot,
rustling and jostling.
One drops your Class of '78 mug
and looks like he may cry when it cracks.

You pat his muscled arm in consolation
and give him another.

After breakfast they take turns with chores.
They rinse dishes, hang the wash,
gape at the revelation that is the vacuum.
One takes a rake and robin-hops
around the yard.

The smallest gives you a rough hug as they leave,
the older two bickering in low-gravel voices.
Come back any time, you say,
and the angels, hungry and humbled
and somehow lost, shake their heads.

#

Frances Klein is an English teacher. She was born and raised in Southeast Alaska, and taught in Bolivia and California before settling in Indianapolis with her husband, Kris. She has been published in several journals, including *GFT Press* and *Autumn Sky Poetry*.

Persephone Hangs Insulation

by Elizabeth Vignali

I cut the batts long, squish them between
beams, a friction fit unfaced by paper.

Lying in the crawlspace, the whole weight
of the house above me. Little lives moving
in the earth beneath my back.

A man-made mineral fiber spun hyacinth
pink, girlish and soft to the touch. Glass
and slag wool and sand ground so fine

you don't notice the itch
at first, the burgeoning burn
stealing the breath from your lungs.

I split another batt, rip from the bottom,
slide half behind and half on top
of the old copper pipes.

Insulation is only
as efficient as the installer.
The key is to fill the void completely.

The lives count down underground, seeds curled
in on themselves against winter's coming breath.
I peel my gloves off and press one hand to the dirt,

the other to the prickling fiberglass. Cold and hot,
a rash of lives, palm pomegranate pink and seeded
with pinpricks of red light, blood rising to the surface.

#

Elizabeth Vignali is an optician and writer in Bellingham, Washington. Her poems have appeared in various publications, including *Willow Springs*, *Crab Creek Review*, *Nimrod*, and *Natural Bridge*. Her chapbook, *Object Permanence*, is available from Finishing Line Press.

Changeling

by Hannah Craig

The house was full of vinegar again.
The walls moved, evaporating into moss.

He had just begun to distinguish shape from shape,
the pang of hunger from the stick of a pin.

Now the woman stood in the door, wearing
her rubber gloves.

And the door filled with that soft yellow gauze
they called *light*.

The walls moved and They came, lifting
him with hands white and long as deer antlers.

The woman, supine on the couch,
her hands like leaping dogs.

They cooed. Claws for faces. Hoof-hearted.
Chick, chick. Luck-duck, chancy child.

Oh, he thought. *So this is wistfulness,* he thought,
looking out and out. Back to the trailer,

to the avenue with its circlets of light.
To the mother, her brow knit with forgetfulness.

To the crib with its shadowy lap, that *something*
so unlucky, still and heavy as a brick.

#

Hannah Craig lives in Pittsburgh, Pennsylvania. Her work has recently appeared in journals like the *Mid-American Review, The Hampden-Sydney Review,* and *Prairie Schooner*. She is the winner of the 2015 New Measure Poetry Prize and her first collection is forthcoming from Parlor Press.

A Water Can Sprays a Flowerbed City

by John Gosslee

outside of the train station

it rains like god is ringing out a towel

the ticket holders bloom umbrellas

drops of water splash into little corsages

I inhale and float up as if a balloon

mismatched flowers pivot on their stems to see

my empty boots fill with cold soup as I ascend

someone's jacket snickers against my pants

a woman yells, *you can't do that!*

she lunges to pluck me down and catches air

#

John Gosslee edits *PANK, Fjords Review* and directs *C&R Press*. His latest work appears in *At Large, Poetry Ireland* and *Prelude*. Johngosslee.com

The Black Dog and Goat

by Forrest DePoy

Streetlights go out along an endless black road

Crunch through leaves, inside the forest you see

The skeleton of a house, much older than bones

Broken glass pops but the woods are silent

The moon is dim but you see a room much darker

A tight bathroom where the wall has fallen out

Blood in the toilet, burnt hair in the sink, and two candles still lit

You follow the song of distant moving planks

The shadows in the corner offer you a mask

They don the black dog, and you the goat

Together you bring a gift fit for a king

The popping and cracking of children roasting

#

Forrest DePoy is a filmmaker for Dirtyfox Productions and a full-time student in Indianapolis. If he isn't busy writing his latest movie script about time-traveling ladybugs, machines that can visualize dreams, or wendigos shadowing their prey, then you can usually find him practicing his writing through short fiction or poetry

Prize Winners Vol. 2

Icons

The Solstice Shade

by F.E. Clark

I saw her again that morning. O'Keeffe—walking away. Always, she was walking away. She didn't look back, never did. I'd tried calling to her, chasing after her—she just slipped away like smoke.

It was one of those summer mornings here in Scotland, when the mists rise and there is still green to shine through. The sky was cerulean and Georgia O'Keeffe—cowboy hat on, clad in black—strode away from the cottage, trailing the scent of wood-smoke and Chanel Number 19 behind her.

I'd been sitting on the step, bare feet on the warm boards, worshipping my morning cup of Jamaican Blue.

Midsummer's day, and the world was brewing fury and hate. Nothing seemed possible. I had not painted in the longest time. My self-imposed isolation wasn't helping. It was telling, of my state of mind, that the shade of the painter visiting me every other morning didn't seem strange.

Seeing the points of a huge rack of antlers jut up dinosaur-like from the ground, I went to investigate.

I wondered what O'Keeffe must make of all this lushness after the adobe and sand, or the vertical cityscapes, of her living-time homes. I knew she must love the foxgloves and honeysuckle, and the lupins and lilies that were thriving here—perhaps they summoned her with their intoxicating scents. The altar began quite by accident, I found a rabbit's foot on my walk in the nearby wood, and luck being in short supply, I'd picked it up. I laid it on the wall on my return. Maybe I had looked to the skies and hollered for some grace—something. A primal scream in the woods—well, why not?

I'd put each bone she brought beside the rabbit's foot, not knowing what to do with them. Every morning, the altar grew, the highlight being the antlers that day—surely a 20-point rack is impossible?

Procrastinating the vastness of a blank canvas I'd pieced the collection of bones together, constructing a chimera skeleton there on the grass—rabbit, bird, sheep, deer, and other bones, strange and impossible to identify. Old and new, smooth and pitted, I held each bone and tried to imagine the flesh and skin and fur that once held them.

That afternoon I made the trip to the village in the old Land Rover with the killer clutch, air-conditioned by way of the cracked windows. I wanted something to toast the solstice and O'Keeffe with, the shop lacked tequila, though perhaps not the worm. They'd sold their only bottle to the "auld dame in black" that morning. I settled on a bottle of Talisker, a single malt from the misty Isle of Skye.

I lit the bonfire at dusk. I'd been saving the wood. It would not get totally dark, the "Simmer Dim" they called in on the islands to the north; that odd light, straight through midnight, that comes at this latitude.

On a whim, I'd set out two camping chairs, two glasses. The fire took immediately, crackling and sparking, scaring off the midgies that had begun to nip at me. White moths and bats whirled in the light.

I poured two tumblers of Talisker. "Here's to you, Georgia," I toasted the empty chair beside me and knocked back the whisky—it burnt. The fire burned. Around me the twilight seemed to vibrate and crackle with electric. I felt the heat from the fire on my face.

I knocked back the second tumbler of whisky, "Here's to the Sun and the Earth and all us stupid buggers who're screwing it up." The whisky had gone to my head. The skirl of bagpipes filled my ears and vibrated in my breastbone.
The rumbling began far away. Grew closer. Louder. CRACK—a log exploded on the fire, spraying sparks. The fire seemed to fill my entire field of vision. It raged. Smoke billowed.

A clattering and clanking came from the grass in front of the cottage—and there, a white beast rose up through the smoke. It staggered to one side, righted itself. Took a step towards me.

I froze. Paralyzed.

The beast cocked its head to one side, tipped its antlers at me, then galloped. Straight at me. Feinting away at the last minute. It circled the bonfire once, then disappeared into the wood.

I glanced to my left and blinked, there on the camping chair was one white blossom—exotic and perfect.

#

F. E. Clark lives in Scotland, where she paints and writes—she is delighted to be here in *The Molotov Cocktail*'s anthology. She is not afraid of the country dark—but does not much care for the dark in the city. A collector of hats, and an avid reader, autumn and spring are her favourite seasons.

The Father of Terror

by Aeryn Rudel

It always starts with the cats.

They show up a few days before a new hole appears, big, muscular black tomcats, slinking through the dark and yowling at the moon. I think they sing to him, maybe to give him the strength to make a new hole. If I let them, they might even make him strong enough to come out of that hole. Then we'd really be fucked.

Of course, convincing the world that a bunch of alley cats are trying to bring back an Egyptian god-demon is a one-way ticket to a padded cell, so my vigil is a lonely one. Each year around the same time, I dream about where the next pit will be. I don't know who sends these visions or whatever; maybe another Egyptian god, a nicer one that doesn't want the world and all us humans on it to be destroyed. The first dream named the thing that could end all things. It's called Abu al-Hol. I found out later that, to the Egyptians, that name meant the "Father of Terror." They even built a monument to it, maybe to keep it from eating them. It's still there, thousands of years later, but everyone calls it the Sphinx now.

The dream came again three nights ago, nearly a week later than last year, and it showed me a place green and wet and cold. I used to get precise locations, like a Google Map in my head, but the last couple of times it's just images. I got lucky; I recognized the place I was being shown, a park in a boring little town outside of Seattle, Washington called Bellevue. So that's where I went, and that's where I'm at now.

Bellevue has one thing going for it—it's wealthy and white. That means no cops, which is good, because the silenced .22 pistol I'm carrying under my rain poncho and the bag of dead cats over my shoulder would be very difficult to explain. I've shot eight cats already. I hate doing it—I *like* cats—but these are different. These are his. I have to kill enough for the ritual that will keep him quiet for another year. The dream told me how to do that, too: what words to say, to use an iron knife instead of a steel one, that kind of thing. It's some kind of magic, and my Christian upbringing says I'm dealing with the devil, but better the devil you know than the one who might come out of a hole and eat the whole fucking world.

There's a lot of parks in Bellevue, and in one of them Abu al-Hol will open his pit. I'm headed there now, working my way through dark streets in the rain, eyes on the lookout for more of his cats. I shoot two more on the way. The Ruger, loaded with subsonic ammo, makes no more than a soft clicking noise when I pull the trigger. That gives me ten. It's enough.

The park is small and secluded, sheltered from the street by lots of trees. There's an empty baseball diamond, sand box, and basketball courts. I know the pit is in the outfield grass. I can smell it—rotten meat and sulfur.

I can see the hole now. It's about six feet across, and wisps of mist or steam rise up from it. It's so black it looks like it was painted on the grass. It's bigger this time.

There are four of his cats around the hole, small dark silhouettes loosing high, wavering cries into the night. I pull the Ruger and snap off two shots. One hits. Three cats race off into the night, and a dead one drops into the hole. That pisses him off. The ground shakes, and I can feel Abu al-Hol's anger in my head like a swarm of bees. Near-paralyzing fear courses through me like bolts of ice. No matter how many times I do this, shut him down, keep him from coming out of the ground, it scares the shit out of me. He isn't called the "Father of Terror" for nothing.

I don't look into the hole as I set my sack on the ground. I did that once, and I'll never do it again. The pit he opens connects to wherever he lives under the ground, and you can see straight down into it. The one time I looked, I saw his eye—slitted, catlike, and the size of the moon—staring up at me. I didn't sleep for a month, and it was the one and only time I've truly considered suicide.

I say the words to the ritual. They don't sound like any language I've ever heard. I've tried sounding them out and writing them down, but even the internet couldn't tell me what they meant.

When I'm done with the words, the ground shakes again, harder. I pick up the bag, open it, and dump the cats on the ground. This is the worst part. I gut each furry body with the iron knife, then toss them into the pit. These are his sacred animals, and throwing their defiled bodies back to him seals the deal. At least that's what I believe. The hole begins to close, and the presence of Abu al-Hol fades from my mind, but he leaves something awful behind, something that cuts the heart from the relief I feel at stopping him one more time. Just before the hole closes completely, Abu al-Hol's rage subsides, and there is something far more terrible behind it: a demon's hope wrapped like serpents around two words.

Next year.

#

Aeryn Rudel is a freelance writer from Seattle, Washington. He is a notorious dinosaur nerd, a rare polearms expert, a baseball connoisseur, and he has mastered the art of fighting with sword-shaped objects (but not actual swords). Aeryn's first novel, *Flashpoint*, was recently published by Privateer Press, and he occasionally offers dubious advice on the subjects of writing and rejection (mostly rejection) on his blog at www.rejectomancy.com.

My Own Private Idol

by Fiona Smith

One of the symptoms of a heart attack is a looming sense of dread.

Fatigue, nausea, lightheadedness, tight-chestedness, shortness of breath, coldness of sweat. Having much in common with your common anxiety attack.

You wander in a pulsing daze. Periphery full of panic spots, nowhere to hide. Shaky at the Whiskey and hyperventilating by the Viper, you take shelter beneath the Mystery Pier Books sign. Better that than the Hollywood sign. That phantom *Land* won't fall off and crush you.

A band should be a gang, they say, full of swagger and mischief—not an anxious small-town androgyne drunkenly recruited by three dough-faced village idiots with a knack for an infectious rock tune. Two slow-sipped beers put in you with an acrid creeping dread are long gone. The crew are well on their way to shitfaced, aka Coolsville. Staying on the straight and narrow makes you more of a child in their eyes. Little do they know what you've taken in your time. When you don't show, they'll piss in your suitcase before they call the cops. No one has your mother's number.

All the common havens of the anxiety-attacked—jacks, corridors, back rooms—are too dank and airless for this bout, too prone to noisy invasion. LA backstreets are too wide, too menacing, so you trip around, flipping through a paltry place-holding stash of confusing low-denomination green notes. You don't know the whereabouts of what tour manager Roy drolly insists on calling your "motel-hotel."

Here to play your treasured bass on a hallowed stage in your black vest and tight jeans, you're a mess. If you survive this sick-fit to make the show, your only urge right now is to scrabble off into those fabled hills, curl up in a ball and expire. Your 19th birthday passed unmarked on the plane. Maybe your mother has a record token in a card for you, propped up like an expectant patient on her mantelpiece. Maybe you're tucked up in your own bed in the idle wilds of your own faraway West and this is a dream about to burst with the dawn chorus.

With every passerby, every nerve-shredding headlight, you feel the heavy-lidded eyes of the group therapy sessions upon you. Sat in silence, dropped off by Mammy, obscure band names and contempt written all over you.

They can tell you think you're far too special and talented to be among them. Every fibre of your being screaming: My pain is less ordinary than yours.

Well, just look at you now, helplessly puking in the parking lot outside the hottest club in the hottest town on the planet.

A side door opens with a burst of heat and noise as someone exits, lights a cigarette.

Hey, he says.

Go away, you whimper into yourself.

Are you okay? he asks, soft, as you shudder, swallow and raise your head but look no further than his lapels. His leather jacket, brown shirt, blue jeans are clean yet they have a dry, dusty aura of something long buried in sand.

You wipe your mouth, spit and glance as far as his chin.

Hundreds of sweating blank faces evaporate into the darkness.

Your synapses fire with recognition. You know that chin. You've seen it a dozen times or more via VCR and cathode ray.

Your pupils widen, light blazes in. Lids snap shut and green flashes pulsate.

Running on empty...

He radiates warmth in your direction, distant concern, blasé curiosity.

Stand by me...

Your eyes find that chin again and you know.

He is risen.

Okay, we are where we are — a lookalike, a surgical sculpting isn't beyond the realms. An actor shooting a biopic of a fallen hero. An uncanny wannabe, showing up at this fateful spot to freak people out, pose for pictures, score free drinks, a walking talking-point.

Another sad fame vulture.

One night in the life...

You glance over towards the Whiskey A Go Go. There's a man in a chicken costume crossing the street and a girl outside in a Batman mask waving a slo-mo sparkler.

You wonder if you've been spiked. You think not yet you have the strangest feeling everyone is moving through a next-door dimension, and time is flowing back and forth through this boulevard like an unstoppable force.

Just breathe, it'll pass, he says.

He breaks out a stick of gum, holds it out.

Peyote in the desert. Swimming upstream.

Slim, slippery LA fairytale. Your American Dream.

Reaching through a dying starlight newborn universe, you take the gum and murmur half-apologies and don't even try to explain that you're from Ireland. You chew chew chew on this magical otherworldly gelatin.

Is this all a special gift from your misfiring brain?

You want to ask him about that night. But it seems so impolite—does he remember how it felt? Floating faces, flashing lights, torch-wielding paramedics, end-of-tunnel brain games? Or just nothingness. And then, what?

Taking in old haunts every night, elbows hovering over shot-soaked bars, fingers lingering on silent guitar strings?

Appearing at sundown outside his favorite 7-Eleven as the pinks fade and the streetlights hum, pockets replenished with cigarettes and gum and the intoxicating favors of shady acquaintances?

You can't say a word to his face, his fringe, downcast eyes and the plume of smoke from his evergreen lips. You just smile at the sight of him, at that peach-fuzz half-grin of his. Zero in on a tiny scorch on his smoking finger you resist the urge to rub.

My slim slight slippery LA fairytale.

Swimming upstream. You jerk back to life, tongue spearing mint.

Your shadowboy is taking his leave, brushing by bouncers, dissolving inside.

You get the distinct impression that where he is going, you are not meant to follow.

You stand upright, brush yourself off, walk slowly back toward the Whiskey, toward that stage.

You can do this.

#

Fiona Smith is a former music journalist working on poetry, short fiction and screenplays. She is from Dublin, Ireland and is a blogger and editor for firstfortnight.ie—the festival of mental health and the arts. Find her on Twitter @fifilebon.

The Further Adventures of Dorothy Gale

by Fred Senese

Her first day back didn't go so well. She'd missed so much. Mr. Seddon asked her to read a poem from the reader. "One who sets reason up for judge of our most holy mystery," she read, but the word *mystery* was one she'd never seen before. All of the other words were black, but this one was in red, like a drop of blood on the page. She dabbed at it and some of it came off, rosy whirls glowing on her fingertip. The other kids laughed when she stopped reading. She heard them whisper: "Musta got hit on the head hard. She got her brains knocked out."

Walking home that afternoon she kept apart from the others. Her lunch basket swinging in her hand as she walked. She was proud of the basket; she'd made it herself. It was a thing she'd brought into the world, all on her own. Well, Mrs. Carter had shown her how to make the God's eye, the diamond weave where the handle meets the bowl. She stopped to look at it again, and she noticed that the glow on her fingertip had faded completely.

God's eye, she thought, that's what they showed me how to do, up there. Only now I can see how people's faces here wrinkle; I can see the hollow gray in their eyes. I can hear their flat words and tik-tok thoughts. I can see how the sky scrapes the earth now.

The little dog ran to her when she opened the gate. She picked him up and squeezed him. He squirmed with delight, licking her hands. She set him down gently. "Go," she said. She couldn't bear to see him now, because he'd been there, too. He was the one person who knew what it was like, and he didn't care where he was, as long as he was with her. He made her feel bad sometimes.

She made a beeline for the hog pen. "Hunk," she said, "I got a problem."

"Shh, girl," he said, "you know she don't like me talking to you, specially not while I'm working." He scraped the coal shovel along the concrete under the trough. It filled with steaming muck. He dumped it into the wheelbarrow and then he stopped, shovel in mid-air, ready for another scrape. "You still here?"

"No," she said.

"Tell me then, sweetie. Be quick."

"Did you ever want something so bad—so much, it's all you can think about. And then you finally get it. And you don't want it anymore."

He smiled. "Can't say as I've ever been in that situation."

"You're lucky, then."

"No," he said. "You're the lucky one. This is all I got, honey. All I ever had the imagination to want. You have everything."

"Everything's not enough."

"I know." He paused. "It was something, that place, huh?"

"I love you so much, Hunk," she said. "You talk to me like it was real."

"It was real enough," he said, "real to you. You got to get back there."

"I don't know how."

"You're growing up," he said. "You know things some people don't figure out all their lives. You'll figure it out."

"I know one thing. I am never going to find my way back there."

"Well. If you can't go back, you got to go forward. You can't think on the things you've left behind. That was your first mistake, wasn't it?"

"Yes," she said, slowly.

"I got to fill this wheelbarrow now. Don't matter what I fill it with. It's the *empty* that's the problem. Now let me get back to it fore I get fired again."

"Thanks. Thank you, Hunk."

"Any time, girl. You remember what I said. Don't you look back next time."

*

Next time started with a man who sold brushes door to door. He dumped her in Texas, a hard, hard place. She got a job waiting tables at the Coney Lunchroom in Houston.

She drew the menu on the chalkboard. The flowers she drew around the margins were the ones she'd known in that far country. She drew them well: red flickered in the chalk when the sun hit it just right.

She bought paper with her tip money and drew on that with chalk and charcoal. The colors bloomed on their own. The owner of the lunchroom hung her drawings up behind the register. Someone asked if they were for sale one day. He said yes. He sold them for five dollars apiece and gave Dorothy fifty cents.

Soon her drawings appeared around the city. Splashes of color in the gray, big red poppies for the stony gray walls of the well-to-do.

A painter from New Orleans bought a drawing and tried to copy it. The colors dripped like mud from his brush. A gallery man saw the drawing tacked to the wall in his studio and bought it for five hundred dollars. When the painter told the gallery man where he'd found it, he drove to Houston that same day. He found her still working in the lunchroom.

When she moved to New Orleans, she painted the moon over Lake Pontchartrain, beating red. She painted the faces of the lost on Bourbon Street in colors no one had ever seen before, the colors of hunter and hunted, wolf howl and tiger paw.

She became known about the city, and then something of a celebrity, and not just in Nola.

She had lovers, one after another. Artists, seers, and magicians, every one.

She never married. She got rich. She put on weight. She acquired a taste for Jamaican coffee, and Jamaican hashish. The color left her hair but never her sight. She painted every day as long as she lived. No one had ever seen anything like the things she painted.

No one will ever see such things again.

She'd have laughed if you told her that. She'd have said that you'll never see anything living backward.

Forward. That's the trick.

#

Fred Senese is a former NASA scientist who teaches at a small university in rural Appalachia. Find him at fredsenese.com, @fsenese on Twitter, and at facebook.com/fredsenesewrites.

Boleskine

by Christopher Stanley

Rain falls helter-skelter before skittering across the murky waters of Loch Ness. Something big ripples towards the southeastern shore. There are monsters here, numerous documented sightings, but the creature emerging from the shallows is broadly that of a middle-aged woman, save for a lingering tail and serpentine tongue. A stray cat hops up onto a gravestone and she breaks its neck, offering it up to Hecate before biting into its abdomen. Blood slithers down her torso and is washed away by the rain until the only remaining trace of the monster is a note of displeasure in the turn of her lips.

Beyond the cemetery, a single-story manor house glows in the moonlight. She remembers calling its name, over and over, the word sounding familiar and foreign at the same time. Boleskine. As she approaches, the iron gates part and flames dance excitedly in the lanterns on either side of the door. Boleskine never returned her calls, not until today.

"Welcome home, my darling rosebud."

His voice comes from both ends of the hallway simultaneously. She should have known better than to imagine he was dead; the rules of mortality have never held firm in this part of Scotland. She hears a baby crying and follows the sound into the sitting room, using an oil lamp to light her way. In the middle of the floor there's a mahogany drinks cabinet, standing tall on claw and ball feet. As she approaches, the doors open to display decanters full of amber escapism and regiments of lead crystal glasses. Her mouth is suddenly dry like the Egyptian desert of her honeymoon.

"You always had weakness for alcohol."

It's been decades since she drank anything other than water from the loch. She touches a glass and it shatters, as does the one next to it. A decanter cracks, sloshing its contents onto the carpet. She steps backwards as the other glasses explode into a million tiny shards. And then the cabinet starts to twist and buckle.

She leaves the room quickly and follows the sound of crying into the dining room. The far wall is covered in oil paintings, five of them, arranged on the points of a pentagram. She reads the names underneath each painting. Mary d'Este Sturges, Jeanne Robert Foster, Roddie Minor, Marie Rohling and Leah Hirsig. She doesn't recognise the names but she knows who they were. His scarlet women, his sacred whores. In the centre of the pentagram is a mirror and in the mirror is a face that hasn't changed in nearly a century.

"You drove me into the arms of other lovers."

Once again she follows the sound of crying, this time into a bedroom decorated with rose-patterned wallpaper. On a sheepskin rug, a cot rocks gently. There's a name engraved into the side panel. Lilith. She approaches the cot, not daring to breathe, hoping against reason for a glimpse of her little girl. But when she steps on the rug, the crying stops. The cot is empty.

"You let our daughter die."

Blinded by tears, she flees the room, tripping and nearly falling through the door. The flickering flame of her oil lamp makes a carnival of the walls. As she steadies herself, she sees something shift in the gloom at the end of the hallway. A tall, robed figure emerges from the shadows, antlers sprouting from its oversized head.

I hated you, Rose Edith Kelly. That's why I made you a monster. That's why I condemned you to the loch."

The creature carefully removes its headpiece, revealing the round, hairless face of her former husband, Aleister Crowley.

"How would you like to see Lilith again?" he asks. "Together we could bring her back."

There's nothing Rose wants more. Crowley beckons her to join him and she steps forward, shivering as his hands slip over her hips.

"My mother called me 'the Beast'," he says, 'and I made you a monster. But you don't have to be a monster anymore. I've forgiven you.'

He pulls her closer until she, too, is engulfed by his black velvet robes and the familiar scents of hashish and sex and magick. She can't remember the last time she felt needed or desired. But she's been here before. While they were married, Crowley exposed her to all manner of madness until she turned to drink. He told her he loved her but he cheated on her and filed for divorce. He dragged her to every unclean corner of the world until their daughter died of typhoid in her arms.

"Let me set you free," he says. "I've been so lonely without you."

Rose lifts the oil lamp up to his face and raises her lips to his ear. "You always made such fantastic promises," she whispers, wondering how quickly his tattered robe would burn. "But I like being a monster."

*

On her way back to the loch, she pauses by a moss-covered headstone and kneels to pay her respects. Boleskine never answered her calls before and it never would again. But sometimes, when she surfaced for air, she would hear a child crying on the southeastern shore.

Her daughter, Lilith. Waiting.

#

Christopher Stanley lives on a hill in South West England, with three sons who share the same birthday but aren't triplets. Various holidays to Scotland have involved trampolining competitions, ironing in the wilderness, and challenging the Loch Ness Monster to umbrellas at dawn. He can be found on Twitter @allthosestrings.

Crumbs

by Gabriel Thibodeau

It started at the park, where we walked along horseshoes of sidewalk and sat for a moment on a little grass hill, and it continued at Olive Garden, where the food isn't really good or bad or Italian or American, but they have those breadsticks. He really loves the breadsticks. I know this because of the way he took a bite and said, "I really love the breadsticks."

We went back to my apartment and sprawled across my bed, side by side at first, sort of overlapped, then in little balls, then crossed over each other: X marks the spot. We looked at the ceiling and each other's faces and the bedspread, and we talked about things, like Sophie's wedding. I told him no, I'm sorry, you can't come. It's going to be really small. I don't have a plus-one. And that's when he turned into a lizard and crawled to the corner of the room.

"Are you okay?" I asked.

"Yep," he said.

"Are you sure?"

"I'm fine." He flicked his lizard tongue. "Why do you ask?"

I sat up on the bedspread. "Because you just turned into a lizard," I said.

He looked at the beige color of my chair and his scales turned beige. "I'm fine," he said again, and then he turned to peer out the window. His head scales looked all windowy.

"Shouldn't we talk about this?" I asked.

"About what?"

"About what's happening right now."

A fly buzzed against the screen. I didn't know what I would do if he ate the fly.

"What's happening?" said the lizard. "Nothing's happening."

He'd asked for extra breadsticks when we'd already finished eating. The waitress slow-walked them to our table with an energy that told me she wished breadsticks had never been invented. He wrapped them in a napkin and ate them in the car on the ride over. There were Parmesan crumbs on my passenger's seat. Now that he was a lizard, I considered going to the garage to vacuum the crumbs. It's hard to know what to do when there's a lizard in the room.

"This is bothering me," I finally said.

"What?"

"This. I'm bothered by this."

He just looked out the window some more, said he had to get going, and crawled away, his scales picking up the blue color of the carpet on his way out. After he left, I stared at the carpet for a while, wondering if he was really still there, just camouflaged, my apartment's secret plus-one.

He called twenty minutes later from his own bedspread, where he always slept alone and diagonally.

"I'm sorry I turned into a lizard," he said.

"The breadsticks aren't even that good," I said.

"They're salty and warm."

"All breadsticks are salty and warm."

I imagined him at Sophie's wedding, a little lizard in a tux. I wondered what color his scales would be. Maybe pink and yellow. Pink and yellow to match the flowers.

#

Gabriel Thibodeau studied English and creative writing at the University of California, Berkeley. He lives in Los Angeles, where he writes stories, produces creative content for award-winning children's products, and pretends to be other people in front of cameras.

The Stories Hadley Hemingway Lost

by Robyn Ryle

In the end, he was glad they were gone. No one wants to be confronted with the stories written in his youth. "Juvenilia," he called them before they disappeared.

The stories boarded the train to Switzerland in a valise. They sat impatient under the seat in the Gare de Lyon station. They were waiting for the whistle and the great bellowing of the train in motion. They were waiting for their chance. They were long-winded and self-indulgent. They were the best work he ever produced. They were doubled, each a twin competing with his carbon copy duplicate. They were his life's work and then they were gone.

They whispered to each other in the darkness. They remembered great stretches of countryside between Michigan and Illinois. Travel was nothing new to them. They grew prophetic and sad as they crossed the border. In the steady rhythm of the train, they could hear the mumbled words of the new stories he would write. Through the window, they watched their replacements rising meteoric as they slid through the Alps. They were small and forgotten.

They wished for nothing more than escape from their confinement. The inside of the valise would never be enough. They longed to drift across the countryside on winds that no words would ever contain. They dreamt of settling down onto fertile soil to rest and decay. They craved the soft touch of rain and snow. Bird nests would be built from their shredded fragments. They would drift down the course of gentle creeks and join with rivers. They would transcend the base physicality of paper and ink.

They would haunt Hemingway's dreams, whole sentences and paragraphs waking him in the tropical heat of Key West and Cuba. In Idaho, their precise phrases rustled around the floorboards of his room in the dark of night. They called to him in familiar voices until the lost stories were all he could hear.

#

Robyn Ryle started life in one small town in Kentucky and ended up in another just down the river in southern Indiana. She teaches sociology to college students when she's not writing. She has a chapbook, *The Face of Baseball*, as well as stories and essays in *CALYX Journal*, *Little Fiction/Big Truths*, *Midwestern Gothic*, *Bartleby Snopes*, and *WhiskeyPaper*, among others. You can find her on Twitter, @RobynRyle.

Visitation

by Allison Spector

    She dresses in blue because it's expected, though nowadays she's more low-key, and angels don't circle overhead with trumpets at her arrival. Instead, the Virgin Mary wears a Persian blue pantsuit and matching work-vest, with a sensible white blouse tucked beneath.
    She worries about her carbon footprint so the Virgin takes public transportation. Tonight, she rides the bus and a red-capped man with a well-groomed mullet eyes her suspiciously. He doesn't trust these foreign women covered with headscarves, whispering Aramaic into their cellphones.
    "I'm watching you," he mouths, pointing a fleshy finger in her direction.
    Mary's shoulders deflate. Her hand traces the neon fabric headrest of the seat in front of her and she says a silent prayer. Above the din of tired conversation, and the rumble of the bus is the strum of a distant viola. In the wake of this sound, the space grows silent. A single white rose sprouts from the fabric where she touched it. Embarrassed, Mary plucks it with her fingers and hides it in her Fendi messenger bag. The man in the

red hat glowers and rests his hand on the concealed pistol beneath his camo jacket.

When the bus nears the Walmart, the Virgin Mary pulls the bell-cord. The halt in momentum causes the passengers to jerk forward, and the Red Cap's gun to slide under his seat. Mary, unbothered, rises to her feet, thanks the bus driver, and braces herself against the evening humidity. Her lungs ache with the detritus of the sultry Southern air.

There used to be a lot of perks to being the Mother of a living god. Mary remembers when she used to manifest on the battlefield in blazing blue splendor. She remembers making bread appear to the orphans of Guadalupe and delivering last rites to popes, heads of state, and Elvis. Today she has a job of a different nature.

Mary loosens her mantle and rolls up her sleeves as she enters the ally. She inhales used cigarette smoke and the smell of stale urine. In the dim evening light, she can discern the shape of a shivering addict with thinning hair and bare feet. A single tear anoints the Virgin's cheek.

A second man sits on a nearby crate, indifferent to the youth suffering in parallel. He pauses in mid-mutter, recognizing Mary's glory. "You should really smile," he croaks as he rises to his feet, blocking her path. But Mary doesn't seem to notice. She brushes past him, fumbles for her employee pass-card, and unlocks the store's back entrance.

Mary slips through the narrow hallway, past the water fountains and the OSHA posters. She reaches out towards the employee locker-rooms. The door swings out in front of her, nearly hitting her in the face.

"You're almost late for the night shift, Mary," her manager says in a cracking voice as he pulls her into his corporate clutches. He rolls his eyes and taps his clipboard. His face is flushed with power and eczema. "Another five minutes and we would have locked you out."

"Mercy is a virtue," the Mother of God replies. She affixes her nametag to her breast, adjusts her cowl, and reaches for her inventory scanner.

"Sure, whatever. Just be more careful." The manager stretches his peach-fuzz lips into an impatient smile. He exits the locker-room and disappears down the hall.

Mary surveys her domain—the church of cheap guns, toxic plastics, and baubles. She hears the click of the locks. Row upon row of lights fade to dimness—a signal that the store is officially closed. Mary begins her task in the shadows. She's been casing the aisles for two weeks, and now it is time to act. She begins with small, obvious items; the scented prayer candles, the religious greeting cards. She touches them gently and indelible family portraits of the Holy Trinity are left behind by her sanctified fingerprints. Mary, the minimalist, knows this is the market that will be the most appreciative, but that she must grace them in moderation. Too many become obvious, tacky. They lose their meaning.

The Holy Mother moves on to Home and Garden. Her face emerges like a stain on the side of a terracotta flowerpot. Next, she visits Menswear and weeps into a torn plastic packet of cotton undershirts. She goes down the Kitchenware aisle. In a moment of divine inspiration, she leaves some lipstick along with her visage on a #1 Mom mug. A velvet painting of her Son will cry real tears. She's feeling cheeky so she leaves it in the aisle with the firearms.

Blankets, bobblehead dolls, wallpaper, baking trays, and mattresses. All of these items receive her divine touch under the pretense of scanning items and stocking shelves. Some young couple on their marital bed will receive a visitation from the Virgin in the form of a holy sweat-stain in the shape of a weeping dove.

Mary checks her smartphone. It's 3:15 a.m. Her shift will soon end. Just one more step on her journey. Footwear. She offers a divine smile to the security cameras before concealing a pair of durable tennis shoes beneath her bright blue vest. She glides back to the employee breakroom and retrieves her messenger bag. Then, without a word she slips out the employee exit. The alarm does not sound. Surveillance records nothing.

The Mother of God hurries as the sky begins to lighten. The barefoot addict coughs silently at the entrance of the alleyway. Mary extends a blue-mantled arm, holding the tennis shoes out by their laces. A thornless white rose is cupped against the left heel. The man stares at her unbelievingly and weeps.

Mary hears the screech of the old city bus. Her legs pump with urgency as she motions for the driver to wait. It's the only way to get to Biloxi this ungodly hour. Mary needs to arrive on time to add her Son's smiling face to a slice of morning toast.

#

Allison Spector is a New Jersey expat who was banished due to a spray-tan allergy. Her work has been published with *1888, Longridge Review, Moonglasses Magazine,* and other fine purveyors of whimsy. You can check out her weird words at allisonspector.com.

Post-Inauguration Day

by Shane Gannaway

    That morning it started raining ash early. The skies had a perma-layer of smog, but the thickness varied, and you could still catch the figure of the sun rising from the east when the veil was thin. At least I figured it was the east. Compasses didn't work anymore and after what happened January 20th, 2017 I wouldn't be surprised if the world was spinning at a completely different angle. I nudged my traveling partner with my foot; he was asleep on the ground, slowly being covered by the falling ash. I went to go stomp out the embers from our campfire the night before. Not that it really mattered. There was nothing remotely close to us that could catch fire. We'd been traveling with kindling and wood on our back. Evening campfires were necessary since every night came with a deadly coldsnap attached. I stared out over the wasteland in front of us. It was identical to what was behind me, what we had traversed previously: miles of flat, gray, scorched earth. No mountains to be seen on the horizon, hardly a hill, and black sticks in the ground for trees. Certainly no sign of human life.

    "Land of the free, all right," Barack Obama said behind me.

I turned. Barry was already up and packed. He was sliding his ski-mask over his eyes as I walked over. I adjusted the scarf around his nose and mouth, and pulled up my own scarf. I didn't have the ski equipment, just a snorkel mask with the nose cut off so I could breathe. It helped keep my scarf in place. Out here the winds could get nasty, and they would generally carry in scorching dust and bits of debris. It was best to keep as much skin covered as possible. I figured I'd let Obama take the better gear. I mean, dude used to be President of the United States, y'know? Also, he was the one who knew where we were going. No working navigational equipment and you could forget about seeing a North Star, but Barry was following something. When I first pressed him about it he would just smile and say, "You wouldn't believe me if I told you."

Eventually he confessed that it was because of a chip implanted just below his left ear. All the presidents had them, he told me. There were exceptions too. Hillary got one, even though she was never technically president. Benjamin Franklin had one too, but that was mostly because he invented them.

"Wasn't gonna not chip himself," Barry chuckled under his breath.

It took a while for me to call Obama anything other than Mr. President, but he kept insisting.

"We're most likely the last two people on this planet. We, uh, might as well have nicknames," he gently explained to me, "for each other. To keep our sanity."

I had to agree. I was never good with nicknames so I just called him Barry. He called me "the Snake," explaining because my name was Sam, and Sam the Snake "sounds cool." I couldn't really argue with that.

We had been traveling for about three hours that morning when Barry held up his hand to signal stop. It felt like for the past week he'd been saying we were close. Maybe this was it.

"This is it," Barack said.

"It is?"

He didn't say "you can trust me" but you could tell he wanted to.

"Now hold on," he kind of mumbled under his breath. He started to remove his scarf and mask.

"Barry, what the hell are you—?"

"Easy now, Snake. I got this. It's gonna be a little unpleasant. Mostly for me." Barry pulled out his knife and stuck it behind his left ear, right where he said the chip was.

"Whoa!" It was all I could say. "Whoa. Barry, do you need—"

He grunted and held a hand back to indicate "stay back." He pried something out of his upper neck and, sure enough, it was some sort of metal object. He clicked something on the chip and it started beeping green. An aggressive wind started to pick up. It was hot, despite the lack of sun, but the flying dirt felt worse than sweat. I pulled my cloak tighter and adjusted my mask. Barry seemed to ignore the wind. He merely dropped the blinking, bloody chip onto the earth. It disappeared instantly, covered in the incoming hot ash.

Nothing happened at first, but after no more than thirty seconds passed a hand exploded from the ground, dust flying high into the air and catching onto the wind making a small twister of sand and dirt. A white, clean-shaven man climbed out of the world. He wore a dark suit and a dark tie; he was predictably filthy. As the man stood there, triumphantly, the mist of debris cleared and I picked him out authoritatively sticking the still-blinking chip into his right ear.

"Sam the Snake," Barry said, covering his bleeding neck with his scarf. "May I introduce D.B. Cooper."

Barry could tell by the look on my face I didn't recognize the name.

"You've never heard of D.B. Cooper?"

"I, uh."

"It's okay, Snake. Before your time, really."

I tried not to look annoyed. It was starting to get dark already. Shade was falling fast over the landscape.

"Well, what'd we have to go all the way out here for? What does D.B do?" I glanced over at Cooper. His eyes were glowing a bright and shimmering green.

"He's our way off this godforsaken planet," Barry said. Cooper gave us two thumbs up and winked at me. I looked skyward. That's why the world was darkening. Descending down towards us was what looked to be some sort of colossal spacecraft. So this must be how we were getting to NATO's Top Secret Moon Base.

Barry looked at me, smiling, and all three of us slowly ascended toward the ship by tractor beam.

#

Shane Gannaway works and lives in Austin, TX. Generally he can be found reading, writing, drinking, or some combination of the three. He is often spotted around town at night looking for ghosts and aliens. Though he hasn't seen any yet, he remains vigilant; he wants to believe.

Trekkie

by Henry Whittier-Ferguson

Mom was a Trekkie, hardcore. She had all the seasons and movies on VHS, and when DVDs came out she bought those as well, and a new TV to watch them on. *Digitally remastered for the twenty-first century*, she'd say. She had the stuff too, the books and posters, the figurines clutching tiny phasers, the scale model ships still in their plastic atmospheres, hovering over the mantel. The rest was in a storage unit that she rented after dad said he wanted all that space crap out of the house.

She had been a hippie, or wanted to be, but she had been born a little late and by then there weren't that many other actual hippies in Tupelo, Mississippi, historical city of gum trees and the birthplace of Elvis, so she told herself it had been a phase, the tie-dye and long blonde braids, the believing in love and peace and humanity united in a transcendental future among the stars. Tupelo's vision of the future was an extension of a present which itself seemed trapped in the past. Before Jayce and I were born, Mom gave tours around the Walk of Life, a path circling Elvis's childhood home. It was comprised of forty-two concrete blocks, one for each year of the King's earthly reign. There was a statue of young Elvis at the thirteenth block to commemorate the year that the Presleys got the fuck outta town, Memphis bound, packed into a '39 Plymouth sedan.

Dad made couches. Specifically, he assembled the wooden frames to which the cushions were eventually stapled. It was a good job. Couches put food on the table. Couches paid for all that space crap. Dad was not a bad man. He liked Buster Keaton and carpentry manuals and did not see the value in literature. *You need to start thinking about your future*, he told me when I turned thirteen, which was his way of saying *get a job*. That night, Mom let us watch *Star Trek II: The Wrath of Khan*.

What stuck in my head was the scene where Khan captures Chekov and Terrell in the desert of Ceti Alpha V and tortures them with brain parasites. *You see, the young enter through the ears and wrap themselves around the cerebral cortex*, says Khan, gesticulating with his forceps, the larvae writhing in his bowl. *This has the effect of rendering the victim extremely susceptible to suggestion. Later, as they grow, follows madness, and death.*

I ended up working on a chicken farm, distributing feed to hens in cages. This involved a quiet resignation on my part, and I came to understand why my father had no patience for imaginings. Jimmy Pickett, the man who owned the chicken farm, refuted evolution, refusing to become just another step on the way to something greater. *I'm the be-all end-all*, he liked to say.

Later, Mom got me a job through her old boss at the Elvis house. I worked the register in the gift shop, selling shot glasses and sweatshirts and shitty little guitars with cheap plastic strings that would snap on the first strum.

The place was a black hole, warping space-time around itself, sucking in human mass and crushing it into a preservative energy. Its density somehow became a negative quantity, a space defined by the birth of the King but characterized by his ultimate absence, and in that way it was a kind of religion. The Presleys' storied exodus constituted an unprecedented launch into the void. Back then, it was said, Memphis musta been six billion light years away.

*

It felt like several lifetimes later that I was living in San Diego and had the idea that I'd fly Mom out and take her to Comic-Con, because she'd never seen the cast in person, and her prognosis was not great. It turned out to be mostly a nightmare, endless lines of costumed naked bodies, but eventually we made our way to the Star Trek area and there was Shatner, a bit sweaty, signing glossy likenesses of himself as a young man.

At that point Mom just wanted to sit down, so we found a spot on the floor and watched him autograph. After a while he took a break. A woman who must have been his assistant brought him a hot dog and he ate it quickly, turning his back to the waiting crowd, licking mustard and relish from his fingers between bites.

Later we drove south around the bay and then back up along the Silver Strand beach, where we pulled the car over to watch the sun melt through that orange California haze into the purple of dusk. Little waves broke against the sand, and the Pacific's vast firmament spread before us, reflecting our light upwards, outwards, into an unimaginable beyond.

#

Henry Whittier-Ferguson is a maker of things with words and sounds and clay. A transplanted Michigander, he studied writing at Lewis & Clark College, and continues to live in Portland, Oregon. You can find more of his work at www.itsthewhat.com.

Prize Winners Vol. 2

The Molotov Cocktail

www.themolotovcocktail.com

The Molotov Cocktail

Prize Winners Vol. 2

Made in the USA
Charleston, SC
30 December 2016